Hannah More

Domestic Tales and Allegories

Illustrating human life

Hannah More

Domestic Tales and Allegories
Illustrating human life

ISBN/EAN: 9783337019792

Printed in Europe, USA, Canada, Australia, Japan

Cover: Foto ©Andreas Hilbeck / pixelio.de

More available books at **www.hansebooks.com**

DOMESTIC TALES

AND

ALLEGORIES;

ILLUSTRATING HUMAN LIFE

I. THE SHEPHERD OF SALISBURY PLAIN.
II. MR. FANTOM.
III. THE TWO SHOEMAKERS.
IV. GILES THE POACHER.
V. THE SERVANT TURNED SOLDIER.
VI. THE GENERAL JAIL DELIVERY.

BY HANNAH MORE

NEW YORK:

D. APPLETON & CO., 90, 92 & 94 GRAND ST.

1869.

NOTICE.

PROBABLY that portion of Hannah More's iteiary works which, when originally published, were most beneficial, and which still are adapted to the most extensive usefulness, is the collection of narratives entitled, "The Cheap Repository Tales." They were designed as antidotes to those demoralizing ballads and fictions which were diffused among the multitudes who have little leisure or inclination for grave meditations. Hence they combine useful instruction in the most familiar form, and inculcate the purest Christian morals, with the exhibition of practical piety, not in the mandatory tone of the didactic monitor, but in the exemplary portraitures of our constant associates, and the actual occurrences of ordinary life.

Two of those Tales only are much known in this country—"All for the Best," and "The Shepherd of Salisbury Plain." The latter has been prefixed, because it is so highly appreciated, and because it unfolds the true character of the whole series.

The Tales are not fictitious, although the homely facts are embellished by the author's imaginative adorning.

But "The Shepherd of Salisbury Plain!" He was not the child of meliorating fiction. Who could behold his healthful, weather-beaten, but placid countenance, his long gray hair, and his white, russet, sheep-like garments, and listen to his prayer and praise, and then forget the lowly but contented and thankful Saunders? The narra or has superadded some circumstances with which he was not encircled; but his domestic habits of life, and his personal traits and social grouping, are sufficiently accurate to embalm the memory of that honest pilgrim, with whom Thomas Wastfield the preacher at Imber associated, although "poor in this world, as rich in faith," and with whom HARVEY's friend STONEHOUSE, immortalized in the " Meditations among the Tombs ;" and by Hannah More as the traveller, Mr. Johnson, delighted to commune during their earthly sojourn, in anticipation of the loftier, deathless fellowship, where the Shepherds of the church, and the Shepherd of the flocks on the plain,

> Now with transporting joys recount
> The labors of their feet.

This volume is published with the assurance, that the reader, after the perusal, will testify that these " Domestic Tales and Allegories," by Hannah More, are equally valuable in their interest and edification.

NEW YORK, *June* 13, 1844.

DOMESTIC

TALES AND ALLEGORIES.

I. THE SHEPHERD OF SALISBURY PLAIN.

MR. JOHNSON, a very worthy charitable gentleman, was travelling some time ago across one of those vast plains which are well known in Wiltshire. It was a fine summer's evening, and he rode slowly that he might have leisure to admire God in the works of his creation. For this gentleman was of opinion, that a walk or a ride was as proper a time as any to think about good things: for which reason, on such occasions, he seldom thought so much about his money, or his trade, or public news, as at other times, that he might with more ease and satisfaction enjoy the pious thought which the wonderful works of the great Maker of heaven and earth are intended to raise in the mind.

As this serene contemplation of the visible heavens insensibly lifted up his mind from the works of God in nature, to the same God as he is seen in Revelation, it occurred to him that this very connexion was clearly intimated by the Royal Prophet in the nineteenth Psalm. That most beautiful description of the greatness and power of God exhibited in the former part, plainly seeming intended to introduce, illustrate, and unfold the operations of the word and Spirit of God on the heart in the latter. And he began to run a parallel in his own mind between the effects of that highly poetical and glowing picture of the material sun in searching and warming the earth. in the first six verses, and the spiritual operation attributed to the "law of God," which fills up the remaining part of the Psalm. And he persuaded himself that the divine Spirit which dictated this fine hymn, had left it as a kind of general intimation to what use we were to convert our admiration of created things; namely, that we might be led by a sight of them to raise our views from the kingdom of nature to that of grace, and that the contemplation of God in his works might draw us to contemplate him in his word.

In the midst of these reflections. Mr. Johnson's attention was all of a sudden called off by the barking of a shepherd's dog, and looking up he spied one of those little huts, which are here and there to be seen on those great downs; and near it was the shepherd himself busily employed with his dog in collecting together his vast flock of sheep. As he drew nearer, he perceived him to be a clean, well-looking, poor man, near fifty years of age. His coat, though at first it had probably been one of dark color, had been in a long course of years so often patched with different sorts of cloth, that it was now become hard to say which had been the original color. But this, while it gave a plain proof of the shepherd's poverty, equally proved the exceeding neatness, industry, and good management of his wife. His stockings no less proved her good house-wifery, for they were entirely covered with darns of different colored worsted, but had not a hole in them; and his shirt, though nearly as coarse as the sails of a ship, was as white as the drifted snow, and was neatly mended where time had either made a rent, or worn it thin. This furnishes a rule of judging, by which one shall seldom be deceived. If I meet with a laborer, hedging, ditching, or mending the highways, with his stockings and shirt tight and whole, however mean and bad his other garments are, I have seldom failed, on visiting his cottage, to find that also clean and well-ordered, and his wife notable, and worthy of encouragement. Whereas a poor woman, who will be lying a-bed, or gossiping with her neighbors when she ought to be fitting out her husband in a cleanly manner, will sel·dom be found to be very good in other respects.

This was not the case with our shepherd ; and Mr. Johnson was not more struck with the decency of his mean and frugal dress, than with his open honest countenance, which bore strong marks of health, cheerfulness, and spirit.

Mr. Johnson, who was on a journey, and some-what fearful from the appearance of the sky, that rain was at no great distance, accosted the shepherd with asking what sort of weather he thought it would be on the morrow. "It will be such weather as pleases me," answered the shepherd. Though the answer was delivered in the mildest and most civil tone that could be imagined, the gentleman thought the words themselves rather rude and surly, and asked him how that could be. "Because," replied the shepherd, "it will be such weather as shall please God, and whatever pleases him always pleases me."

Mr. Johnson, who delighted in good men and good things, was very well satisfied with his reply. For he justly thought that though a hypocrite may easily contrive to appear better than he really is to a stranger ; and that no one should be too soon trusted, merely for having a few good words in his mouth ; yet as he knew that out of the abundance of the heart the mouth speaketh, he always accustomed himself to judge favorably of those who had a serious deport-ment and solid manner of speaking. It looks as if it proceeded from a good habit, said he, and though I may now and then be deceived by it, yet it has not often happened to me to be so. Whereas if a man accosts me with an idle, dissolute, vulgar, indecent, or profane expression I have never been deceived in

him, but have generally on inquiry found his character to be as bad as his language gave me room to
expect.

He entered into conversation with the shepherd in
the following manner: "Yours is a troublesome life,
honest friend," said he. "To be sure, sir," replied
the shepherd, "'tis not a very lazy life; but 'tis not
near so toilsome as that which my GREAT MASTER
led for my sake; and he had every state and condition
of life at his choice, and *chose* a hard one; while I
only submit to the lot that is appointed to me." "You
are exposed to great cold and heat," said the gentleman: "True sir," said the shepherd; "but then I
am not exposed to great temptations; and so throwing
one thing against another, God is pleased to contrive
to make things more equal than we poor, ignorant,
short-sighted creatures are apt to think. David was
happier when he kept his father's sheep on such a
plain as this, and employed in singing some of his
own Psalms perhaps, than ever he was when he became king of Israel and Judah. And I dare say we
should never have had some of the most beautiful
texts in all those fine Psalms, if he had not been a
shepherd, which enabled him to make so many fine
comparisons and similitudes, as one may say, from
country life, flocks of sheep, hills and valleys, fields
of corn, and fountains of water."

"You think, then," said the gentleman, "that a
laborious life is a happy one." "I do, sir; and more
so especially, as it exposes a man to fewer sins. If
King Saul had continued a poor laborious man to the
end of his days, he might have lived happy and honest, and died a natural death in his bed at last, which
you know, sir, was more than he did. But I speak
with reverence, for it was divine Providence over-
ruled all that, you know, sir, and I do not presume to
make comparisons. Besides, sir, my employment has
been particularly honored—Moses was a shepherd in
the plains of Midian. It was to "shepherds keeping

their flocks by night" that the angels appeared in Bethlehem, to tell the best news, the gladdest tidings, that ever were revealed to poor sinful men ; often and often has the thought warmed my poor heart in the coldest night, and filled me with more joy and thankfulness than the best supper could have done."

Here the shepherd stopped, for he began to feel that he had made too free, and talked too long. But Mr. Johnson was so well pleased with what he said, and with the cheerful contented manner in which he said it, that he desired him to go on freely, for that it was a pleasure to him to meet with a plain man, who, without any kind of learning but what he had got from the Bible, was able to talk so well on a subject in which all men, high and low, rich and poor, are equally concerned.

" Indeed I am afraid I make too bold, sir, for it better becomes me to listen to such a gentleman as you seem to be, than to talk in my poor way : but as I was saying, sir, I wonder all working men do not derive as great joy and delight as I do from thinking how God has honored poverty ! Oh ! sir, what great, or rich, or mighty men have had such honor put on them, or their condition, as shepherds, tent-makers, fishermen, and carpenters have had ? Beside, it seems as if God honored industry also. The way of duty is not only the way of safety, but it is remarkable how many in the exercise of the common duties of their calling, humbly and rightly performed, as we may suppose, have found honors, preferment, and blessing ; while it does not occur to me that the whole sacred volume presents a single instance of a like blessing conferred on idleness. Rebekah, Rachel, and Jethro's daughters, were diligently employed in the lowest occupations of a country life, when Providence, by means of those very occupations, raised them up husbands so famous in history, as Isaac, Jacob, and the prophet Moses. The shepherds were neither playing nor sleeping, but " watching their

flocks," when they received the news of a Savior's
birth : and the woman of Samaria, by the laborious
office of drawing water, was brought to the knowledge of Him who gave her to drink of " living
water."

"My honest friend," said the gentleman, "I per-
ceive you are well acquainted with scripture." " Yes,
sir, pretty well, blessed be God ! through his mercy
I learned to read when I was a little boy; though
reading was not so common when I was a child, as, I
am told, through the goodness of Providence and the
generosity of the rich, it is likely to become now-a-
days. I believe there is no day for the last thirty
years that I have not peeped at my Bible. If we
can't find time to read a chapter, I defy any man to
say he can't find time to read a verse : and a single
text, sir, well followed, and put in practice every day,
would make no bad figure at the year's end; three
hundred and sixty-five texts, without the loss of a
moment's time, would make a pretty stock, a little
golden treasury, as one may say, from new-year's
day to new-year's day ; and if children were brought
up to it, they would come to look for their text as
naturally as they do for their breakfast. No laboring
man, 'tis true has so much leisure as a shepherd, for
while the flock is feeding I am obliged to be still,
and at such times I can now and then tap a shoe for
my children or myself, which is a great saving to
us, and while I am doing that I repeat a chapter or a
psalm, which makes the time pass pleasantly in this
wild solitary place. I can say the best part of the
New Testament by heart; I believe I should not say
the best part, for every part is good, but I mean the
greatest part. I have led but a lonely life, and have
often had but little to eat, but my Bible has been
meat, drink, and company to me, as I may say, and
when want and trouble have come upon me, I don't
know what I should have done indeed, sir, if I had

not had the promises of this book for my stay and
support "

"You have had great difficulties then?" said Mr
Johnson. "Why, as to that, sir, not more than
neighbor's fare; I have but little cause to complain,
and much to be thankful; but I have had some little
struggles, as I will leave you to judge. I have a wife
and eight children, whom I bred up in that little cottage which you see under the hill, about half a mile
off." "What, that with the smoke coming out of
the chimney?" said the gentleman. "O no, sir,"
replied the shepherd, smiling, "we have seldom
smoke in the evening, for we have little to cook, and
firing is very dear in these parts. 'Tis that cottage
which you see on the left hand of the church, near
that little tuft of hawthorns."—"What, that hovel
with only one room above and below, with scarcely
any chimney? how is it possible that you can live
there with such a family?" "O it is very possible,
and very certain too," cried the shepherd. "How
many better men have been worse lodged! how many
good Christians have perished in prisons and dungeons, in comparison of which my cottage is a
palace! The house is very well, sir; and if the
rain did not sometimes beat down upon us through
the thatch when we are a-bed, I should not desire a
better; for I have health, peace, and liberty, and no
man maketh me afraid."

"Well, I will certainly call on you before it be
long, but how can you contrive to lodge so many
children?" "We do the best we can, sir. My poor
wife is a very sickly woman; or we should always
have done tolerably well. There are no gentry in
the parish, so that she has not met with any great
assistance in her sickness. The good curate of the
parish, who lives in that pretty parsonage in the val-.
ley, is very willing, but not very able to assist us on
these trying occasions, for he has little enough for
himself, and a large family into the bargain. Yet he

does what he can, and more than many other men do, and more than he can well afford. Beside that, his prayers and good advice we are always sure of, and we are truly thankful for that, for a man must give you know sir, according to what he hath, and not according to what he hath not."

"I am afraid," said Mr. Johnson, "that your difficulties may sometimes lead you to repine."

"No, sir," replied the shepherd, "it pleases God to give me two ways of bearing up under them. I pray that they may be either removed or sanctified to me. Beside, if my road be right I am contented, though it be rough and uneven. I do not so much stagger at hardships in the right way, as I dread a false security, and a hollow peace, while I may be walking in a more smooth, but less safe way. Beside, sir, I strengthen my faith by recollecting what the best men have suffered, and my hope, with the view of the shortness of all suffering. It is a good hint, sir, of the vanity of all earthly possessions, that though the whole Land of Promise was his, yet the first bit of ground which Abraham, the father of the faithful, got possession of, in the land of Canaan, was a *grave*.

"Are you in any distress at present?" said Mr. Johnson. "No, sir, thank God," replied the shepherd "I get my shilling a-day, and most of my children will soon be able to earn something: for we have only three under five years old."—"Only!" said the gentleman, "that is a heavy burden."—"Not at at all; God fits the back to it. Though my wife is not able to do any out-of-door work, yet she breeds up our children to such habits of industry, that our little maids, before they are six years old, can first get a half-penny, and then a penny a day by knitting. The boys, who are too little to do hard work, get a trifle by keeping the birds off the corn; for this the farmers will give them a penny or two pence, and now and then a bit of bread and cheese into the bargain.

When the season of crow-keeping is over, then they glean or pick stones ; anything is better than idleness, sir, and if they did not get a farthing by it, I would make them do it just the same, for the sake of giving them early habits of labor.

" So you see, sir, I am not so badly off as many are ; nay, if it were not that it costs me so much in 'pothecary's stuff for my poor wife, I should reckon myself well off, nay I do reckon myself well off ; for blessed be God, he has granted her life to my prayers. and I would work myself to a 'natomy, and live on one meal a day, to add any comfort to her valuable life ; indeed I have often done the last, and thought it no great matter neither."

While they were in this part of the discourse, a fine, plump, cherry-cheek little girl ran up out of breath, with a smile on her young happy face, and without taking any notice of the gentleman, cried out with great joy—"Look here, father, only see how much I have got !" Mr. Johnson was much struck with her simplicity, but puzzled to know what was the occasion of this great joy. On looking at her he perceived a small quantity of coarse wool, some of which had found its way through the holes of her clean but scanty and ragged woollen apron. The father said, " This has been a successful day indeed, Molly, but don't you see the gentleman?" Molly now made a courtesy down to the very ground ; while Mr. Johnson inquired into the cause of mutual sat- isfaction which both father and daughter had ex pressed, at the unusual good fortune of the day.

" Sir," said the shepherd, " poverty is a great sharpener of the wits—My wife and I can not endure to see our children, poor as they are, without shoes and stockings, not only on account of the pinching cold which cramps their poor little limbs, but because it degrades and debases them ; and poor people who have but little regard to appearances, will seldom be found to have any great regard for honesty and good-

2

ness; I don't say this is always the case; but I am
sure it is so too often. Now shoes and stockings
being very dear, we could never afford to get them
without a little contrivance. I must show you how
I manage about the shoes when you condescend to
call at our cottage, sir; as to stockings, this is one
way we take to help to get them. My young ones,
who are too little to do much work, sometimes wan-
der at odd hours over the hills for the chance of finding what little wool the sheep may drop when they
rub themselves, as they are apt to do against the
bushes. These scattered bits of wool the children
pick out of the brambles, which I see have torn sad
holes in Molly's apron to-day; they carry this wool
home, and when they have got a pretty parcel together, their mother cards it; for she can sit and card
in the chimney corner, when she is not able to wash
or work about house. The biggest girl then spins
it; it does very well for us without dying, for poor
people must not stand for the color of their stockings.
After this our little boys knit it for themselves, while
they are employed in keeping cows in the fields, and
after they get home at night. As for the knitting
which the girls and their mother do, that is chiefly for
sale, which helps to pay our rent."

Mr. Johnson lifted up his eyes in silent astonish-
ment, at the shifts which honest poverty can make
rather than beg or steal; and was surprised to think
now many ways of subsisting there are, which those
who live at their ease little suspect. He secretly resolved to be more attentive to his own petty expenses
than he had hitherto been; and to be more watchful
that nothing was wasted in his family.

But to return to the shepherd. Mr. Johnson told
him that as he must needs be at his friend's house,
who lived many miles off, that night, he could not, as
he wished to do, make a visit to his cottage at present.
" But I will certainly do it," said he, " on my return,
for I long to see your wife and her nice little family,
and to be an eyewitness of her neatness and good

management. The poor man's tears started into his eyes on hearing the commendation bestowed on his wife; and wiping them off with the sleeve of his coat, for he was not worth a handkerchief in the world, he said—"Oh sir, you just now, I am afraid, called me an humble man, but indeed I am a very proud one."—"Proud!" exclaimed Mr. Johnson, "I hope not—Pride is a great sin, and as the poor are liable to it as well as the rich, so good a man as you seem to be, ought to guard against it."—"Sir," said he, "you are right, but I am not proud of myself, God knows I have nothing to be proud of. I am a poor sinner, but indeed, sir, I am proud of my wife; she is not only the most tidy, notable woman on the plain, but she is the kindest wife and mother, and the most contented, thankful Christian that I know. Last year I thought I should have lost her, in a violent fit of the rheumatism, caught by going to work too soon after her lying-in, I fear; for 'tis but a bleak coldish place, as you may see, sir, in winter, and sometimes the snow lies so long under the hill, that I can hardly make myself a path to get out and buy a few necessaries in the next village; and we are afraid to send out the children, for fear they should be lost when the snow is deep. So, as I was saying, the poor soul was very bad indeed, and for several weeks lost the use of all her limbs except her hands; a merciful Providence spared her the use of these, so that when she could not turn in her bed, she could contrive to patch a rag or two for her family. She was always saying, had it not been for the great goodness of God, she might have had her hands lame as well as her feet, or the palsy instead of the rheumatism, and then she could have done nothing—but, nobody had so many mercies as she had.

"I will not tell you what we suffered during that bitter weather, sir, but my wife's faith and patience during that trying time, were as good a lesson to me as any sermon I could hear, and yet Mr. Jenkins gave us very comfortable ones, too, that helped to keep up my spirits."

"I fear, shepherd," said Mr. Johnson, "you have found this to be but a bad world."

"Yes, sir," replied the shepherd, "but it is governed by a good God. And though my trials have now and then been sharp, why then, sir, as the saying is, if the pain be violent, it is seldom lasting, and if it be but moderate, why then we can bear it the longer, and when it is quite taken away, ease is the more precious, and gratitude is quickened by the remembrance; thus every way, and in every case, I can always find out a reason for vindicating Providence."

"But," said Mr. Johnson, "how do you do to support yourself under the pressure of actual want. Is not hunger a great weakener of your faith?"

"Sir," replied the shepherd, "I endeavor to live upon the promises. You who abound in the good things of this world are apt to set too high a value on them. Suppose, sir, the king, seeing me hard at work, were to say to me, that, if I would patiently work on till Christmas, a fine palace and a great estate should be the reward of my labors. Do you think, sir, that a little hunger, or a little wet would make me flinch, when I was sure that a few months would put me in possession! Should I not say to myself frequently—Cheer up, shepherd, 'tis but till Christmas! Now is there not much less difference between this supposed day and Christmas, when I should take possession of the estate and palace, than there is between time and eternity, when I am sure of entering on a kingdom not made with hands? There is some comparison between a moment and a thousand years, because a thousand years are made up of moments, all time being made up of the same sort of stuff, as I may say; while there is no sort of comparison between the longest portion of time and eternity. You know, sir, there is no way of measuring two things, one of which has length and breadth, which shows it must have an end somewhere, and another thing which being eternal, is without end and without measure."

"But," said Mr. Johnson, " is not the fear of death sometimes too strong for your faith?"

"Blessed be God, sir," replied the shepherd, " the dark passage through the valley of the shadow of death, is made safe by the power of Him who conquered death. I know, indeed, we shall go as naked out of this world as we came into it, but an humble penitent will not be found naked in the other world, sir. My Bible tells me of garments of praise and robes of righteousness. And is it not a support, sir, under any of the petty difficulties and distresses here, to be assured by the word of Him who can not lie, that those who were in white robes came out of tribulation! But, sir, I beg your pardon for being so talkative. Indeed, you great folks can hardly imagine how it raises and cheers a poor man's heart, when such as you condescend to talk familiarly to him on religious subjects. It seems to be a practical comment on that text which says, *the rich and the poor meet together, the Lord is the maker of them all.* And so far from creating disrespect, sir, and that nonsensical wicked notion about equality, it rather prevents it. But to turn to my wife. One Sunday afternoon when she was at the worst, as I was coming out of church, for I went one part of the day, and my eldest daughter the other, so my poor wife was never left alone; as I was coming out of church, I say, Mr. Jenkins, the minister, called out to me and asked me how my wife did, saying he had been kept from coming to see her by the deep fall of snow, and indeed from the parsonage-house to my hovel, it was quite impassable. I gave him all the particulars he asked, and, I am afraid, a good many more, for my heart was quite full. He kindly gave me a shilling, and said he would certainly try to pick out his way and come and see her in a day or two.

" While he was talking to me a plain farmer-look
ing gentleman in boots, who stood by, listened to all 1
said, but seemed to take no notice. It was Mr. Jenkins' wife's father, who was come to pass the Christmas holydays at the parsonage-house. I had always
heard him spoken of as a plain frugal man, who lived
close himself, but was remarked to give away more
han any of his show-away neighbors.

" Well! I went home with great spirits at this
seasonable and unexpected supply ; for we had tap-
ped our last sixpence, and there was little work to be
had on account of the weather. I told my wife I
had not come back empty-handed.—' No. 1 dare say
not,' says she, you have been serving a Master, *who
filleth the hungry with good things, though he sendeth
the rich empty away.'* True ; Mary, says I, we seldom fail to get good spiritual food from Mr. Jenkins,
but to-day he has kindly supplied our bodily wants.
She was more thankful when I showed her the shilling, than, I dare say, some of your great people are
when they get a hundred pounds."

Mr. Johnson's heart smote him when he heard
such a value set upon a shilling ; " surely," said he to
himself, " I will never waste another ;" but he said
nothing to the shepherd, who thus pursued his story.

" Next morning before I went out, I sent part of
the money to buy a little ale and brown sugar to put
into her water-gruel, which made it nice and nourish-
ing. I went out to cleave wood in a farm-yard, for
there was no standing out on the plain, after such
snow as had fallen in the night. I went with a lighter
heart than usual, because I had left my poor wife a
little better, and comfortably supplied for this day,
and I now resolved more than ever to trust God for
the supplies of the next. When I came back at
night, my wife fell a crying as soon as she saw me.
This, I own, I thought but a bad return for the blessings she had so lately received, and so I told her. 'Oh,'
said she, ' it is too much, we are too rich; I am now

frightened, not lest we should have no portion in this world, but for fear we should have our whole portion in it. Look here, John!' So saying, she uncovered the bed whereon she lay, and showed me two warm, thick, new blankets. I could not believe my own eyes, sir, because when I went out in the morning, I had left her with no other covering than our little old, thin, blue rug. I was still more amazed when she put half a crown into my hand, telling me she had had a visit from Mr. Jenkins and Mr. Jones, the latter of whom had bestowed all these good things upon us. Thus, sir, have our lives been crowned with mercies. My wife got about again, and I do believe, under Providence, it was owing to these comforts; for the rheumatism, sir, without blankets by night, and flannel by day, is but a baddish job, especially to people who have little or no fire. She will always be a weakly body; but, thank God, her soul prospers and is in health. But I beg your pardon, sir, for talking on at this rate." " Not at all, not at all," said Mr. Johnson; " I am much pleased with your story, you shall certainly see me in a few days. Good night." So saying, he slipped a crown into his hand and rode off. " Surely," said the shepherd, " *goodness and mercy have followed me all the days of my life*," as he gave the money to his wife when he got home at night.

As to Mr. Johnson, he found abundant matter for his thoughts during the rest of his journey. On the whole, he was more disposed to envy than to pity the shepherd. " I have seldom seen," said he, " so happy a man. It is a sort of happiness which the world could not give, and which I plainly see, it has not been able to take away. This must be the true spirit of religion. I see more and more, that true goodness is not merely a thing of words and opinions, but a living principle brought into every common action of a man's life. What else could have supported this poor couple under every bitter trial of want and sickness? No, my honest shepherd, I do not pity, but I respect and even honor thee; and I will visit thy poor hovel on my return to Salisbury, with as much pleasure as I am now going to the house of my friend."

Mr. Johnson, after having passed some time with his friend, set out on his return to Salisbury, and on the Saturday evening reached a very small inn, a mile or two distant from the shepherd's village; for he never travelled on a Sunday without such a reason as he might be able to produce at the day of judgment. He went the next morning to the church nearest the house where he had passed the night; and after taking such refreshment as he could get at that house, he walked on to find out the shepherd's cottage. His reason for visiting him on a Sunday was chiefly because he supposed it to be the only day which the shepherd's employment allowed him to pass at home with his family; and as Mr. Johnson had been struck with his talk, he thought it would be neither unpleasant nor unprofitable to observe how a man who carried such an appearance of piety spent his Sunday: for though he was so low in the world, this gentleman was not above entering very closely into his character, of which he thought he should be able to form a better judgment, by seeing whether his practice at home kept pace with his professions abroad: for it is not so much by observing how people talk, as how they live, that we ought to judge of their characters.

After a pleasant walk, Mr. Johnson got within sight of the cottage, to which he was directed by the clump of hawthorns and the broken chimney. He wished to take the family by surprise: and walking gently up to the house, he stood awhile to listen. The door being half open, he saw the shepherd (who looked so respectable in his Sunday coat that he should hardly have known him), his wife, and their numerous young family, drawing round their little table, which was covered with a clean, though very coarse cloth. There stood on it a large dish of potatoes, a brown pitcher, and a piece of a coarse loaf. The wife and children stood in silent attention, while the shepherd, with uplifted hands and eyes, devoutly begged the blessing of Heaven on their homely fare. Mr. Johnson could not help sighing to reflect, that he had sometimes seen better dinners eaten with less appearance of thankfulness.

The shepherd and his wife sat down with great seeming cheerfulness, but the children stood; and while the mother was helping them, little fresh-colored Molly, who had picked the wool from the bushes with so much delight, cried out, "Father, I wish I was big enough to say grace, I am sure I should say it very heartily to-day, for I was thinking what must *poor* people do who have no salt to their potatoes; and do but look, our dish is quite full."—"That is the true way of thinking, Molly," said the father; "in whatever concerns bodily wants and bodily comforts, it is our duty to compare our own lot with the lot of those who are worse off, and that will keep us thankful: on the other hand, whenever we are tempted to set up our own wisdom or goodness, we must compare ourselves with those who are wiser and better, and that will keep us humble." Molly was now so hungry, and found the potatoes so good, that she had no time to make any more remarks, but was devouring her dinner very heartily, when the barking of the great dog drew her attention from her trencher to the door, and spying the stranger, she cried out, "Look, father, see here, if yonder is not the good gentleman!" Mr. Johnson finding himself discovered, immediately walked in, and was heartily welcomed by the honest shepherd, who told his wife that this was the gentleman to whom they were so much obliged.

The good woman began, as some very neat people are rather apt to do, with making many apologies that her house was not cleaner, and that things were not in a fitter order to receive such a gentleman. Mr. Johnson, however, on looking round, could discover nothing but the most perfect neatness. The trenchers on which they were eating, were almost as white as their linen; and notwithstanding the number and smallness of the children, there was not the least appearance of dirt or litter. The furniture was very simple and poor, hardly indeed amounting to bare necessaries. It consisted of four brown wooden chairs, which, by constant rubbing, were become as bright as a looking-glass; an iron pot and kettle; a poor old grate, which scarcely held a handful of coal, and out of which the little fire that had been in it appeared to have been taken, as soon as it had answered the end for which it had been lighted—that of boiling their potatoes. Over the chimney stood an old-fashioned, broad, bright candlestick, and a still brighter spit: it was pretty clear that this last was kept rather for ornament than use. An old carved elbow chair, and a chest of the same date, which stood in the corner, were considered the most valuable part of the shepherd's goods, having been in his family for three generations. But all these were lightly esteemed by him in comparison of another possession, which, added to the above, made up the whole of what he had inherited from his father, and which last he would not have parted with, if no other could have been had, for the king's ransom; this was a large old Bible, which lay on the window-seat, neatly covered with brown cloth, variously patched. This sacred book was most reverently preserved from dog's ears, dirt, and every other injury, but such as time and much use had made it suffer in spite of care. On the clean white walls was pasted, a hymn on the Crucifixion of our Savior, a print of the Prodigal Son, the Shepherd's Hymn, a *New History of a True Book*, and Patient Joe, or the Newcastle Collier.

After the first salutations were over, Mr. Johnson said, that if they would go on with their dinner he would sit down. Though a good deal ashamed, they thought it more respectful to obey the gentleman,

who having cast his eye on their slender provisions,
gently rebuked the shepherd for not having indulged
himself, as it was Sunday, with a morsel of bacon to
relish his potatoes.   The shepherd said nothing, but
poor Mary colored and hung down her head, saying,
" Indeed, sir, it is not my fault, I did beg my husband
to allow himself a bit of meat to-day out of your
honor's bounty; but he was too good to do it, and it
is all for my sake."   The shepherd seemed unwilling
to come to an explanation, but Mr. Johnson desired
Mary to go on.   So she continued: " You must
know, sir, that both of us, next to a sin, dread a debt,
and indeed, in some cases a debt is a sin; but with all
our care and pains, we have never been able quite to
pay off the doctor's bill for that bad fit of rheumatism
which I had last winter.   Now, when you were
pleased to give my husband that kind present the
other day, I heartily desired him to buy a bit of meat
for Sunday, as I said before, that he might have a
little refreshment for himself out of your kindness.
But,' answered he, ' Mary, it is never out of my
mind long together that we still owe a few shillings
to the doctor, and, thank God, it is all we did owe in
the world.   Now, if I carry him this money directly,
it will not only show him our honesty and our good-
will, but it will be an encouragement to him to come
to you another time, in case you should be taken
once more in such a bad fit; for I must own,' added
my poor husband, ' that the thought of your being so
terribly ill without any help, is the only misfortune
that I want courage to face.' "
Here the grateful woman's tears ran down so fast
that she could not go on.   She wiped them with the
corner of her apron, and humbly begged pardon for
making so free.   " Indeed, sir," said the shepherd,
" though my wife is full as unwilling to be in debt as
myself, yet I could hardly prevail on her to consent
to my paying this money just then, because she said
it was hard that I should not have a taste of the gen-

tleman's bounty myself. But for once, sir, I would
have my own way. For you must know, as I pass the
best part of my time alone, tending my sheep, 'tis a
great point with me, sir, to get comfortable matter for
my own thoughts ; so that 'tis rather self-interest in
me to allow myself in no pleasures and no practices
that won't bear thinking on over and over. For when
one is a good deal alone, you know, sir, all one's bad
deeds do so rush in upon one, as I may say, and so
torment one, that there is no true comfort to be had
but in keeping clear of wrong doings and false pleasures; and that I suppose may be one reason why so
many folks hate to stay a bit by themselves. But, as
I was saying, when I came to think the matter over
on the hill yonder. said I to myself. 'A good dinner is
a good thing, I grant. and yet it will be but cold comfort to me a week after, to be able to say—to be sure.
I had a nice shoulder of mutton last Sunday for dinner, thanks to the good gentleman! but then I am in
debt. I *had* a rare dinner, that's certain; but the
pleasure of that has long been over, and the debt still
remains. I have spent the crown ; and now if my
poor wife should be taken in one of those fits again,
die she must, unless God work a miracle to prevent
it, for I can get no help for her.' This thought settled all ; and I set off and paid the doctor with as
much cheerfulness as I should have felt on sitting
down to the fattest shoulder of mutton that ever was
roasted. And if I was contented at the time, think
how much more happy I have been at the remembrance! O sir, there are no pleasures worth the name,
but such as bring no plague or penitence after them."

Mr. Johnson was satisfied with the shepherd's reasons, and agreed that though a good dinner was not
to be despised, yet it was not worthy to be compared
with *a contented mind, which* (as the Bible truly says)
is a continual feast. "But come," said the good gentleman, "what have we got in this brown mug ?"
'As good water," said the shepherd. "as any in the

king's dominions. I have heard of countries beyond sea, in which there is no wholesome water; nay, I have been myself in a great town not far off, where they are obliged to buy all the water which they get, while a good Providence sends to my very door a spring as clear and fine as Jacob's well. When I am tempted to repine that I have often no other drink, I call to mind that it was nothing better than a cup of cold water which the woman at the well of Sychar drew for the greatest guest that ever visited this world."

"Very well," replied Mr. Johnson; "but as your honesty has made you prefer a poor meal to being in debt, I will at least send and get something for you to drink. I saw a little public house just by the church, as I came along. Let that little rosy-faced fellow fetch a mug of beer." So saying, he looked full at the boy, who did not offer to stir, but cast an eye at his father to know what he was to do. "Sir," said the shepherd, "I hope we shall not appear ungrateful if we seem to refuse your favor; my little body would, I am sure, fly to serve you on any other occasion. But, good sir, it is Sunday, and should any of my family be seen at a public house on a Sabbath day, it would be a much greater grief to me than to drink water all my life. I am often talking against these doings to others; and if I should say one thing and do another, you can't think what an advantage it would give many of my neighbors over me, who would be glad enough to report that they had caught the shepherd's son at the alehouse, without explaining how it happened. Christians, you know, sir, must be doubly watchful, or they will not only bring disgrace on themselves, but what is much worse, on that holy name by which they are called."

"Are you not a little too cautious, my honest friend?" said Mr. Johnson. "I humbly ask your pardon, sir," replied the shepherd, "if I think that is impossible. In my poor notion I no more understand how a man can be too cautious, than how he can be too strong or too healthy."

"You are right, indeed," said Mr. Johnson, "as a general principle, but this struck me as a very small thing." "Sir," said the shepherd, "I am afraid you will think me very bold, but you encourage me to speak out." "'Tis what I wish," said the gentleman. "Then, sir," resumed the shepherd, "I doubt if, where there is a frequent temptation to do wrong, any fault can be called small; that is, in short, if there is any such thing as a small wilful sin. A poor man like me is seldom called out to do great things, so that it is not by a few striking deeds his character can be judged by his neighbors, but by the little round of daily customs he allows himself in."

"I should like," said Mr. Johnson, "to know how you manage in this respect."

"I am but a poor scholar, sir," replied the shepherd, "but I have made myself a little sort of rule. I always avoid, as I am an ignorant man, picking out any one single difficult text to distress my mind about, or to go and build opinions upon, because I know that puzzles and injures poor unlearned Christians. But I endeavor to collect what is the *general* spirit or meaning of Scripture on any particular subject, by putting a few texts together, which, though I find them dispersed up and down, yet all seem to look the same way, to prove the same truth, or hold out the same comfort. So when I am tried or tempted, or any thing happens in which I am at a loss what to do, I apply to my rule—to the *law and the testimony.* To be sure I can't always find a particular direction as to the very case, because then the Bible must have been bigger than all those great books I once saw in the library at Salisbury palace, which the butler told me were acts of parliament; and had that been the case, a poor man would never have had money to buy, nor a working man time to read the Bible; and so Christianity could only have been a religion for the rich, for those who had money and leisure, which, blessed be God! is so far from being the truth, that in all that fine discourse of our Savior to John's disciples, it is enough to reconcile any poor man in the world to his low condition, to observe, when Christ reckons up the things for which he came on earth, to observe, I say, what he keeps for last. *Go tell John*, says he, *those things which ye do hear and see; the blind receive their sight, and the lame walk, the lepers are cleansed, and the deaf hear, and the dead are raised up.* Now sir, all these are wonders, to be sure, but they are nothing to what follows. They are but like the lower rounds of a ladder, as I may say, by which you mount to the top—*and the poor have the gospel preached to them.* I dare say if John had any doubts before, this part of the message must have cleared them up at once. For it must have made him certain sure at once, that a religion which placed preaching salvation to the poor above healing the sick, which ranked the soul above the body, and set heaven above health, must have come from God.''

'' But,'' said Mr. Johnson, ''you say you can generally pick out your particular duty from the Bible, though that immediate duty be not fully explained.''

'' Indeed, sir,'' replied the shepherd, ''I think I can find out the principle, at least, if I bring but a willing mind. The want of that is the great hinderance. *Whoso doeth my will, he shall know of the doctrine.* You know that text, sir. I believe a stubborn will makes the Bible harder to be understood than any want of learning. 'Tis corrupt affections which blind the understanding, sir. The more a man hates sin, the clearer he will see his way, and the more he loves holiness, the better he will understand his Bible—the more practical conviction will he get of that pleasant truth, that *the secret of the Lord is with them that fear him.* Now, sir, suppose I had time and learning, and possessed of all the books I saw at the bishop's, where could I find out a surer way to lay the axe to the root of all covetousness, selfishness, and injustice, than the plain and ready rule, *to do unto all men as I would they should do unto me.* If my neighbor does me an injury, can I be at any loss how to proceed with him, when I recollect the parable of the unforgiving steward, who refused to pardon a debt of a hundred pence, when his own ten thousand talents had been remitted to him? I defy any man to retain habitual selfishness, hardness of heart, or any other allowed sin, who daily and conscientiously tries his own heart by this touchstone. The straight rule will show the crooked practice to every one who honestly tries the one by the other."

"Why, you seem to make Scripture a thing of general application," said Mr. Johnson, "in cases in which many, I fear, do not apply."

"It applies to everything, sir," replied the shepherd. "When those men who are now disturbing the peace of the world, and trying to destroy the confidence of God's children in their Maker and their Savior—when those men, I say, came to my poor hovel with their new doctrines and their new books, I would never look into one of them; for I remember it was the first sin of the first pair to lose their innocence for the sake of a little wicked knowledge; besides, *my own book* told me—*To fear God and honor the king—To meddle not with them who are given to change—Not to speak evil of dignities—To render honor to whom honor is due.* So that I was furnished with a little coat-of-mail, as I may say, which preserved me, while those who had no such armor fell into the snare."

While they were thus talking, the children, who had stood very quietly behind, and had not stirred a foot, now began to scamper about all at once, and in a moment ran to the window-seat to pick up their little old hats. Mr. Johnson looked surprised at this

disturbance ; the shepherd asked his pardon, telling
him it was the sound of the church bell which had
been the cause of their rudeness; for their mother
had brought them up with such a fear of being too
late for church, that it was but who could catch the
first stroke of the bell, and be first ready. He had
always taught them to think that nothing was more
indecent than to get into church after it was begun ;
for as the service opened with an exhortation to repentance, and a confession of sin, it looked very pre-
sumptuous not to be ready to join it ; it looked as if
people did not feel themselves to be sinners. And
though such as lived at a great distance might plead
difference of clocks as an excuse, yet those who
lived within the sound of the bell could pretend neither ignorance nor mistake.

Mary and her children set forward. Mr. Johnson
and the shepherd followed, taking care to talk the
whole way on such subjects as might fit them for the
solemn duties of the place to which they were going.
"I have often been sorry to observe," said Mr. Johnson, "that many who are reckoned decent, good kind
of people, and who would on no account neglect
going to church, yet seem to care but little in what
frame or temper of mind they go thither. They will
talk of their worldly concerns till they get within the
door, and then take them up again the very minute
the sermon is over, which makes me ready to fear
they lay too much stress on the mere form of going
to a place of worship. Now, for my part, I always
find that it requires a little time to bring my mind
into a state fit to do any *common* business well, much
more this great and most necessary business of all."
" Yes, sir," replied the shepherd, " and then I think,
too, how busy I should be in preparing my mind, if
I were going into the presence of a great gentleman,
or a lord, or the king; and shall the King of kings be
treated with less respect ? Besides, one likes to see
people feel as if going to church was a thing of

choice and pleasure, as well as a duty, and that they were as desirous not to be the last there, as they would be if they were going to a feast or a fair."

After service, Mr. Jenkins, the clergyman, who was well acquainted with the character of Mr. Johnson, and had a great respect for him, accosted him with much civility, expressing his concern that he could not enjoy just now so much of his conversation as he wished, as he was obliged to visit a sick person at a distance, but hoped to have a little talk with him before he left the village. As they walked along together, Mr. Johnson made such inquiries about the shepherd as served to confirm him in the high opinion he entertained of his piety, good sense, industry, and self-denial. They parted—the clergyman promising to call in at the cottage on his way home.

The shepherd, who took it for granted that Mr. Johnson was gone to the parsonage, walked home with his wife and children, and was beginning in his usual way to catechise and instruct his family, when Mr. Johnson came in and insisted that the shepherd should go on with his instructions just as if he were not there. This gentleman, who was very desirous of being useful to his own servants and workmen in the way of religious instruction, was sometimes sorry to find that though he took a good deal of pains, they now and then did not quite understand him; for though his meaning was very good, his language was not always very plain, and though the *things* he said were not hard to be understood, yet the *words* were, especially to such as were very ignorant. And he now began to find out that if people were ever so wise and good, yet if they had not a simple, agreeable, and familiar way of expressing themselves, some of their plain hearers would not be much the better for them. For this reason he was not above listening to the plain, humble way in which this honest man taught his family; for though he knew that he himself had many advantages over the shepherd, had

more learning, and could teach him many things, yet
he was not too proud to learn even of so poor a man,
in any point where he thought the shepherd might
have the advantage of him.

This gentleman was much pleased with the knowledge and piety which he discovered in the answers of
the children ; and desired the shepherd to tell him
how he contrived to keep up a sense of divine things
in his own mind, and in that of his family, with so
little leisure, and so little reading. " Oh! as to that,
sir," said the shepherd, " we do not read much except in one book, to be sure ; but with my heart
prayer for God's blessing on the use of that book,
what little knowledge is needful seems to come of
course, as it were. And my chief study has been to
bring the fruits of the Sunday reading into the week's
business, and to keep up the same sense of God in the
heart when the Bible is in the cupboard, as when it
is in the hand. In short, to apply what I read in the
book to what I meet with in the field."

" I don't quite understand you," said Mr. Johnson.
" Sir," replied the shepherd, " I have but a poor gift at
conveying these things to others, though I have much
comfort from them in my own mind ; but I am sure
that the most ignorant and hard-working people, who
are in earnest about their salvation, may help to keep
up devout thoughts and good affections during the
week, though they have hardly any time to look at a
book ; and it will help them to keep out bad thoughts
too, which is no small matter. But then they must
know the Bible ; they must have read the word of
God diligently ; that is a kind of stock in trade for a
Christian to set up with ; and it is this which makes
me so careful in teaching it to my children, and even
in storing their memories with psalms and chapters.
This is a great help to a poor, hard-working man,
who will scarcely meet with anything in them but
what he may turn to some good account. If one lives
in the fear and love of God, almost everything one

sees abroad will teach one to adore his power and goodness, and bring to mind some text of Scripture, which shall fill his heart with thankfulness, and his mouth with praise. When I look upward, *the heavens declare the glory of God*, and shall I be silent and ungrateful? If I look round and see the valleys standing thick with corn, how can I help blessing that Power who *giveth me all things richly to enjoy?* I may learn gratitude from the beasts of the field, for the *ox knoweth his owner and the ass his master's crib;* and shall a Christian not know, shall a Christian not consider what great things God has done for him? I, who am a shepherd, endeavor to fill my soul with a constant remembrance of that good Shepherd, *who feedeth me in green pastures, and maketh me to lie down beside the still waters, and whose rod and staff comfort me.* A religion, sir, which has its seat in the heart, and its fruits in the life, takes up little time in the study: and yet in another sense, true religion, which from sound principles bringeth forth right practice, fills up the whole time, and life too, as one may say.

"You are happy," said Mr. Johnson, "in this retired life, by which you escape the corruptions of the world." "Sir," replied the shepherd, "I do not escape the corruptions of my own evil nature. Even there, on that wild solitary hill, I find out that my heart is prone to evil thoughts. I suppose, sir, that different states have different temptations. You great folks that live in the world, perhaps, are exposed to some, of which such a poor man as I am, knows nothing. But to one who leads a lonely life like me, evil thoughts are a chief-besetting sin; and I can no more withstand these without the grace of God, than a rich gentleman can withstand the snares of evil company, without the same grace. And I find that I stand in need of God's help continually; and if he should give me up to my own evil heart, I should be lost."

Mr. Johnson approved of the shepherd's sincerity.

for he had always observed, that where there was no humility, and no watchfulness against sin, there was no religion, and he said that the man who did not feel himself to be a sinner, in his opinion could not be a Christian.

Just as they were in this part of their discourse, Mr. Jenkins the clergyman came in. After the usual salutations, he said, " Well, shepherd, I wish you joy ; I know you will be sorry to gain any advantage by the death of a neighbor ; but Old Wilson, my clerk, was so infirm, and I trust so well prepared, that there is no reason to be sorry for his death. I have been to pray by him, but he died while I stayed. I have always intended you should succeed to his place ; 'tis no great matter of profit, but every little is something.

" No great matter, sir !" cried the shepherd ; "indeed, it is a great thing to me ; it will more than pay my rent. Blessed be God for all his goodness !"— Mary said nothing, but lifted up her eyes full of tears in silent gratitude.

" I am glad of this little circumstance," said Mr. Jenkins, " not only for your sake, but for the sake of the office itself. I so heartily reverence every religious institution, that I would never have even the *amen* added to the prayers of our church, by vain or profane lips ; and if it depended on me, there should be no such thing in the land as an idle, drunken, or irreligious parish clerk. Sorry I am to say that this matter is not always sufficiently attended to, and that I know some of a very indifferent character.

Mr. Johnson now inquired of the clergyman whether there were many children in the parish. " More than you would expect," replied he, " from the seeming smallness of it ; but there are some little hamlets which you do not see."—"I think," returned Mr. Johnson, " I recollect that in the conversation which I had with the shepherd on the hill yonder, he told me you had no Sunday school "—"I am sorry to say we have none," said the minister. "I do what I can to remedy this misfortune by public catechising; but having two or three churches to serve, I can not give so much time as I wish to private instruction; and having a large family of my own, and no assistance from others, I have never been able o establish a school."

" There is an excellent institution in London," said Mr. Johnson, "called the Sunday-school Society, which kindly gives books and other helps, on the application of such pious clergymen as stand in need of their aid, and which I am sure would have assisted you, but I think we shall be able to do something ourselves. "Shepherd," continued he, "if I were a king, and had it in my power to make you a rich and a great man, with a word speaking, I would not do it. Those who are raised, by some sudden stroke, much above the station in which Divine Providence had placed them, seldom turn out very good, or very happy. I have never had any great things in my power, but as far as I have been able, I have been always glad to assist the worthy. I have, however, never attempted or desired to set any poor man much above his natural condition, but it is a pleasure to me to lend him such assistance as may make that condition more easy to himself, and put him in a way which shall call him to the performance of more duties than perhaps he could have performed without my help, and of performing them in a better manner to others, and with more comfort to himself.—What rent do you pay for this cottage?"

" Fifty shillings a year, sir."

" It is in a sad tattered condition; is there not a better to be had in the village?"

" That in which the poor clerk lived," said the clergyman, "is not only more tight and whole, but has two decent chambers, and a very large light kitchen."—"That will be very convenient," replied Mr. Johnson, "pray, what is the rent?"—"I think, said the shepherd, "poor Neighbor Wilson gave somewhat about four pounds a year, or it might be guineas."—"Very well," said Mr. Johnson, "and what will the clerk's place be worth, think you?" "About three pounds," was the answer.

"Now," continued Mr. Johnson, 'my plan is that the shepherd should take that house immediately; for as the poor man is dead, there will be no need of waiting till quarter-day, if I make up the difference.' "True, sir," said Mr. Jenkins, "and I am sure my wife's father, whom I expect to-morrow, will willingly assist a little toward buying some of the clerk's old goods. And the sooner they remove the better; for poor Mary caught that bad rheumatism by sleeping under a leaky thatch." The shepherd was too much moved to speak, and Mary could hardly sob out, "Oh, sir! you are too good; indeed, this house will do very well." "It may do very well for you and your children, Mary," said Mr. Johnson, gravely, "but it will not do for a school; the kitchen is neither large nor light enough. Shepherd," continued he, "with your good minister's leave, and kind assistance, I propose to set up in this parish a Sunday school, and to make you the master. It will not at all interfere with your weekly calling, and it is the only lawful way in which you could turn the Sabbath into a day of some little profit to your family, by doing, as I hope, a great deal of good to the souls of others. The rest of the week you will work as usual. The difference of rent between this house and the clerk's I shall pay myself; for to put you in a better house at your own expense, would be no great act of kindness. As for honest Mary, who is not fit for hard labor, or any other out-of-door work, I propose to endow a small weekly school, of which she shall be the mistress, and employ her notable turn to good account, by teaching ten or a dozen girls to knit, sew, spin, card, or any other useful way of getting their bread; for all this I

shall only pay her the usual price, for I am not going
to make you rich, but useful."

"Not rich, sir!" cried the shepherd; "How can I
ever be thankful enough for such blessings? And
will my poor Mary have a dry thatch over her head?
and shall I be able to send for the doctor when I am
like to lose her? Indeed, my cup runs over with
blessings: I hope God will give me humility." Here
he and Mary looked at each other and burst into tears.
The gentlemen saw their distress, and kindly walked
out upon the little green before the door, that these
honest people might give vent to their feelings. As
soon as they were alone, they crept into one corner
of the room, where they thought they could not be
seen, and fell on their knees, devoutly blessing and
praising God for his mercies. Never were more
hearty prayers presented, than this grateful couple
offered up for their benefactors. The warmth of their
gratitude could only be equalled by the earnestness
with which they besought the blessing of God on the
work in which they were going to engage.

The two gentlemen now left this happy family, and
walked to the parsonage, where the evening was
spent in a manner very edifying to Mr. Johnson, who
the next day took all proper measures for putting the
shepherd in immediate possession of his now comfort
able habitation. Mr. Jenkins's father-in-law, the wor
thy gentleman who gave the shepherd's wife the
blankets, arrived at the parsonage before Mr. Johnson
left it, and assisted in fitting up the clerk's cottage.

Mr. Johnson took his leave, promising to call on
the worthy minister and his new clerk once a year, in
his summer's journey over the plain, as long as it
should please God to spare his life. He had every
reason to be satisfied with the objects of his bounty.
The shepherd's zeal and piety made him a blessing
to the rising generation. The old resorted to his
school for the benefit of hearing the young instructed;
and the clergyman had the pleasure of seeing that he

was rewarded for the protection he gave the school, by the great increase in his congregation. The shepherd not only exhorted both parents and children to the indispensable duty of a regular attendance at church, but by his pious counsels he drew them thither, and by his plain and prudent instructions enabled them to understand, and of course, to delight in the public worship of God.

4

II. HISTORY OF MR. FANTOM,

THE NEW-FASHIONED PHILOSOPHER,

AND HIS MAN WILLIAM.

MR. FANTOM was a retail trader in the city of London. As he had no turn to any expensive vices, he was reckoned a sober, decent man; but he was covetous and proud, selfish and conceited. As soon as he got forward in the world, his vanity began to display itself, though not in the ordinary method, that of making a figure and living away; but still he was tormented with a longing desire to draw public notice, and to distinguish himself. He felt a general sense of discontent at what he was, with a general ambition to be something which he was not: but this desire had not yet turned itself to any particular object. It was not by his money he could hope to be distinguished, for half his acquaintance had more, and a man must be rich, indeed, to be noted for his riches in London. Mr. Fantom's mind was a prey to his vain imaginations. He despised all those little acts of kindness and charity which every man is called to perform every day, and while he was contriving grand schemes, which lay quite out of his reach, he neglected the ordinary duties of life which lay directly before him. Selfishness was his governing principle. He fancied he was lost in the mass of general society, and the usual means of attaching importance to insignificance occurred to him—that of getting into clubs and societies. To be connected with a party

would at least make him known to that party, be it
ever so low and contemptible; and this local importance it is which draws off vain minds from those
scenes of general usefulness, in which, though they
are of more value, they are of less distinction.

About this time he got hold of a famous little book
written by the NEW PHILOSOPHER, whose pestilent
doctrines have gone about seeking whom they may
destroy. These doctrines found a ready entrance
into Mr. Fantom's mind, a mind at once shallow and
inquisitive, speculative and vain, ambitious and dissat-
isfied. As almost every book was new to him, he
fell into the common error of those who begin to
read late in life—that of thinking that what he did
not know himself was equally new to others; and
he was apt to fancy that he and the author he was
reading were the only two people in the world who
knew anything. This book led to the grand discov-
ery; he had now found what his heart panted after—
a way to *distinguish himself.* To start out a full-
grown philosopher at once, to be wise without education, to dispute without learning, and to make
proselytes without argument, was a short cut to
fame which well suited his vanity and his ignorance.
He rejoiced that he had been so clever as to examine
for himself, pitied his friends who took things upon
trust, and was resolved to assert the freedom of his
own mind. To a man fond of bold novelties and
daring paradoxes, solid argument would be flat and
truth would be dull, merely because it is not new.
Mr. Fantom believed, not in proportion to the strength
of the evidence, but to the impudence of the asser-
tion. The trampling on holy ground with dirty
shoes, the smearing the sanctuary with filth and
mire, the calling the prophets and apostles by the
most scurrilous names was new, and dashing, and
dazzling. Mr. Fantom, now being set free from the
chains of slavery and superstition, was resolved to
show his zeal in the usual way by trying to free

others; but it would have hurt his vanity had he
known that he was the convert of a man who had
written only for the vulgar, who had *invented* nothing,
no, not even one idea of original wickedness, but
who had stooped to take up out of the kennel of in
fidelity all the loathsome dregs and offal dirt which
politer unbelievers had thrown away as too gross and
offensive for the better bred readers.

Mr. Fantom, who considered that a philosopher
must set up with a little sort of stock in trade, now
picked up all the commonplace notions against Christianity, which have been answered a hundred times
over; these he kept by him ready cut and dried, and
brought out in all companies with a zeal which would
have done honor to a better cause, but which the
friends to a better cause are not so apt to discover.
He soon got all the cant of the new school. He
prated about *narrowness*, and *ignorance*, and *bigotry*,
and *prejudice*, and *priestcraft*, on the one hand, and on
the other, of *public good*, the *love of mankind*, and
liberality, and *candor*, and *toleration*, and above all,
benevolence. Benevolence, he said, made up the
whole of religion, and all the other parts of it were
nothing but cant, and jargon, and hypocrisy. By
benevolence he understood a gloomy and indefinite
anxiety about the happiness of people with whom he
was utterly disconnected, and whom Providence had
put it out of his reach either to serve or injure. And
by the happiness this benevolence was so anxious to
promote, he meant an exemption from the power of
the laws, and an emancipation from the restraints of
religion, conscience, and moral obligation.

Finding, however, that he made little impression
on his old club at the Cat and Bagpipes, he grew
tired of their company. This club consisted of a
few sober citizens, who met of an evening for a little
harmless recreation after business; their object was,
not to reform parliament, but their own shops; not
to correct the abuses of government but of parish

officers; not to cure the excesses of administration but of their own porters and apprentices; to talk over the news of the day without aspiring to direct the events of it. They read the papers with that anxiety which every honest man feels in the daily history of his country. But as trade which they *did* understand, flourished, they were careful not to reprobate those public measures by which it was protected, and which they did *not* understand. In such turbulent times it was a comfort to each to feel he was a tradesman and not a statesman, that he was not called to responsibility for a trust for which he found he had no talents, while he was at full liberty to employ the talents he really possessed in fairly amassing a fortune, of which the laws would be the best guardian, and government the best security. Thus a legitimate self-love, regulated by prudence and restrained by principle, produced peaceable subjects and good citizens, while in Fantom a boundless selfishness and inordinate vanity converted a discontented trader into a turbulent politician.

There was, however, one member of the Cat and Bagpipes whose society he could not resolve to give up, though they seldom agreed, as indeed no two men in the same class and habits of life could less resemble each other. Mr. Trueman was an honest, plain, simple-hearted tradesman of the good old cut, who feared God and followed his business; he went to church twice on Sundays, and minded his shop all the week, spent frugally, gave liberally, and saved moderately. He lost, however, some ground in Mr. Fantom's esteem because he paid his taxes without disputing, and read his Bible without doubting.

Mr. Fantom now began to be tired of everything in trade except the profits of it, for the more the word benevolence was in his mouth the more did selfishness gain dominion in his heart. He, however, resolved to retire for a while into the country, and devote his time to his new plans, schemes, theories,

and projects for the public good. A life of talking,
and reading, and writing, and disputing, and teaching,
and proselyting, now struck him as the only life, so
he soon set out for the country with his family, for
unhappily Mr. Fantom had been the husband of a
very worthy woman many years before the new philosophy had discovered that marriage was a shameful
infringement on human liberty, and an abridgement
of the rights of man.   To this family was now added
his new footman, William Wilson, whom he had
taken with a good character out of a sober family.
Mr. Fantom was no sooner settled than he wrote to
invite Mr. Trueman to come and pay him a visit, for
he would have burst if he could not have got some
one to whom he might display his new knowledge·
he knew that if on the one hand Trueman was no
scholar, yet on the other he was no fool ; and though
he despised his *prejudices*, yet he thought he might
be made a good decoy duck, for if he could once
bring Trueman over, the whole club at the Cat and
Bagpipes might be brought to follow his example,
and thus he might see himself at the head of a society of his own proselytes—the supreme object of a
philosopher's ambition.   Trueman came accordingly.
He soon found that however he might be shocked at
the impious doctrines his friend maintained, yet that
an important lesson might be learned even from the
worst enemies of truth, namely, an ever-wakeful attention to their grand object. · If they set out with
talking of trade or politics, of private news or public
affairs, still Mr. Fantom was ever on the watch to
hitch in his darling doctrines ; whatever he began
with he was sure to end with a pert squib at the Bible, a vapid jest on the clergy, the miseries of super
stition, and the blessings of philosophy.   " Oh," said
Trueman to himself, " when shall I see Christians
half so much in earnest?   Why is it that almost all
zeal is on the wrong side ?"

   " Well, Mr Fantom," said Trueman, one day a-

breakfast, "I am afraid you are leading but an idle
sort of life here." " Idle, sir!" said Fantom, "I now
first begin to live to some purpose; I have indeed lost
too much time, and wasted my talents on a little retail trade in which one is of no note; one can't distinguish one's self." " So much the better," said Trueman, " I had rather not distinguish myself, unless it
was by leading a better life than my neighbors.
There is nothing I should dread more than being
talked about. I dare say now heaven is in a good
measure filled with people whose names were never
heard of out of their own street and village. So I beg
leave not to distinguish myself!" " Yes, but one
may, if it is only by signing one's name to an essay
or paragraph in a newspaper," said Fantom. " Heav-
en keep John Trueman's name out of a newspaper,"
interrupted he in a fright, "for if it be there it must
either be found in the Old Bailey or the bankrupt
list, unless, indeed, I were to remove shop, or sell off
my old stock. Well, but Mr. Fantom, you, I suppose, are now as happy as the day is long?" "O
yes," replied Fantom, with a gloomy sigh, which
gave the lie to his words, "perfectly happy! I wonder you do not give up all your sordid employments,
and turn philosopher!" " Sordid, indeed!" said Trueman; " do not call names, Mr. Fantom, I shall never
be ashamed of my trade. What is it has made this
country so great? a country whose merchants are
princes? It is trade, Mr. Fantom, trade. I can not
say indeed, as well as I love business, but now and
then, when I am overworked, I wish I had a little
more time to look after my soul; but the fear that I
should not devote the time, if I had it, to the best
purpose, makes me work on, though often, when I
am balancing my accounts, I tremble lest I should
neglect to balance the grand account. But still, since.
like you, I am a man of no education, I am more
afraid of the temptations of leisure than of those of
business; I never was bred to read more than a

chapter in the Bible, or some other good book, or the magazine and newspaper, and all that I can do now, after shop is shut, is to take a walk with my children in the field besides. But if I had nothing to do from morning to night, I might be in danger of turning politician or philosopher. No, neighbor Fantom, depend upon it that where there is no learning, next to God's grace, the best preservative of human virtue is business. As to our political societies, like the armies in the cave of Adullam, 'every man that is in distress, and every man that is in debt, and every man that is discontented, will always join themselves unto them.' "

Fantom. You have narrow views, Trueman. What *can* be more delightful than to see a paper of one's own in print against tyranny and superstition, contrived with so much ingenuity, that, though the law is on the lookout for treason and blasphemy, a little change of name defeats its scrutiny. For instance, you may stigmatize *England* under the name of *Rome,* and *Christianity* under that of *Popery.* The true way is to attack whatever you have a mind to injure under another name, and the best means to destroy the use of a thing, is to produce a few incontrovertible facts against the abuses of it. Our late travellers have inconceivably helped on the cause of the new philosophy in their ludicrous narratives of credulity, miracles, indulgences, and processions, in popish countries, all which they ridicule under the broad and general name of religion, Christianity, and *the church.* "And are not you ashamed to defend such knavery?" said Mr. Trueman. "Those who have a great object to accomplish," replied Mr. Fantom, " must not be nice about the means. But to return to yourself, Trueman ; in your little confined situation you can be of no use." "That I deny," interrupted Trueman ; "I have filled all the parish offices with some credit , I never took a bribe at an election, no, not so much as a treat ; I take care of my apprentices, and do not set them a bad example by running to plays and Sadler's Wells in the week, or jaunting about in a gig all day on Sundays; for I look upon it that the country jaunt of the master on Sunday exposes his servants to more danger than their whole week's temptation in trade put together."

Fantom. I once had the same vulgar prejudices about the church and the Sabbath, and all that antiquated stuff. But even on your own narrow principles, how can a thinking being spend his Sunday better (if he must lose one day in seven by having any Sunday at all) than by going into the country to admire the works of nature.

Trueman. I suppose you mean the works of God for I never read in the Bible that Nature made anything. I should rather think that she herself was made by Him, who, when he said, " Thou shalt not murder," said also, " Thou shalt keep holy the sabbath-day." But now do you really think that all that multitude of coaches, chariots, chaises, vis-a-vis, booby-hutches, sulkies, sociables, phætons, gigs, curricles, cabrioles, chairs, stages, pleasure-carts, and horses, which crowd our roads—all those country-houses within reach, to which the London friends pour in to the gorgeous Sunday feast, which the servants are kept from church to dress—all those public houses under the signs of which you read these alluring words, *an ordinary on Sundays;* I say, do you really believe that all those houses and carriages are crammed with philosophers, who go on Sunday into the country to admire the works of nature, as you call it! Indeed, from the reeling gait of some of them when they go back at night, one might take them for a certain sect called the tippling philosophers. Then in answer to your charge, that a little tradesman can do no good, it is not true; I must tell you that I belong to the Sick Man's Friend, and to the Society for relieving Prisoners for Small Debts.

Fantom. I have no attention to spare to that busi

ness, though I would pledge myself to produce a plan by which the *national* debt might be paid off in six months; but all yours are petty occupations.

Trueman. Then they are better suited to petty men of petty fortune. I had rather have an ounce of real good done with my own hands, and seen with my own eyes, than speculate about doing a ton in a wild way, which I know can never be brought about.

Fantom. I despise a narrow field. O for the reign of universal benevolence! I want to make all mankind good and happy.

Trueman. Dear me! sure that must be a wholesale sort of a job; had you not better try your hand at a town or a parish first!

Fantom. Sir, I have a plan in my head for relieving the miseries of the whole world. Everything is bad as it now stands. I would alter all the laws, and do away all the religions, and put an end to all the wars in the world. I would everywhere redress the injustice of fortune, or what the vulgar call Providence. I would put an end to all punishments; I would not leave a single prisoner on the face of the globe. This is what I call doing things on a grand scale. "A scale with a vengeance," said Trueman. "As to releasing the prisoners, however, I do not so much like that, as it would be liberating a few rogues at the expense of all honest men; but as to the rest of your plans, if all Christian countries would be so good as to turn Christians, it might be helped on a good deal. There would be still misery enough left indeed; because God intended this world should be earth and not heaven. But, sir, among all your oblations, you must abolish human corruption before you can make the world quite as perfect as you pretend. You philosophers seem to me to be ignorant of the very first seed and principle of misery—sin, sir, sin; your system of reform is radically defective; for it does not comprehend that sinful nature from which all misery proceeds. You accuse government of de-fects which belong to man, to individual man, and of course to man collectively. Among all your reforms you must reform the human heart; you are only hacking at the branches without striking at the root. Banishing impiety out of the world would be like striking off all the pounds from an overcharged bill; and all the troubles which would be left would be reduced to mere shillings, pence, and farthings, as one may say."

Fantom. Your project would rivet the chains which mine is designed to break.

Trueman. Sir, I have no projects. Projects are in general the offspring of restlessness, vanity, and idleness. I am too busy for projects, too contented for theories, and, I hope, have too much honesty and humility for a philosopher. The utmost extent of my ambition at present is to redress the wrongs of a parish apprentice who has been cruelly used by his master: Indeed, I have another little scheme, which is to prosecute a fellow in our street who has suffered a poor wretch in a workhouse, of which he had the care, to perish through neglect, and you must assist me.

Fantom. The parish must do that. You must not apply to me for the redress of such petty grievances. I own that the wrongs of the Poles and South Americans so fill my mind as to leave me no time to attend to the petty sorrows of workhouses and parish apprentices. It is provinces, empires, continents, that the benevolence of the philosopher embraces; every one can do a little paltry good to his next neighbor.

Trueman. Every one can, but I do not see that every one does. If they would, indeed, your business would be ready done at your hands, and your grand ocean of benevolence would be filled with the drops which private charity would throw into it. I am glad, however, you are such a friend to the prisoners, because I am just now getting a little subscription from our club, to set free our poor old friend Tom

Saunders, a very honest brother tradesman, who go
first into debt, and then into jail, through no fault of
his own, but merely through the pressure of the
times. We have each of us allowed a trifle every
week toward maintaining Tom's young family since
he has been in prison; but we think we shall do much
more service to Saunders, and indeed in the end light-
en our own expense, by paying down at once a little
sum to restore him to the comforts of life, and put
him in a way of maintaining his family again. We
have made up the money all except five guineas. I
am already promised four, and you have nothing to
do but give me the fifth. And so, for a single guinea,
without any of the trouble, the meetings, and the
looking into his affairs, which we have had—which,
let me tell you, is the best, and to a man of business,
the dearest part of charity—you will at once have the
pleasure (and it is no small one) of helping to save a
worthy family from starving, of redeeming an old friend
from jail, and of putting a little of your boasted benevolence into action. Realize! Master Fantom:
there is nothing like realizing. " Why, hark ye, Mr.
Trueman," said Fantom, stammering, and looking
very black, " do not think I value a guinea: no, sir,
I despise money; it is trash; it is dirt, and beneath
the regard of a wise man. It is one of the unfeeling
inventions of artificial society. Sir, I could talk to
you for half a day on the abuse of riches, and on my
own contempt of money."

Trueman. O pray do not give yourself the trouble;
it will be an easier way by half of vindicating yourself from one, and of proving the other, just to put
your hand in your pocket and give me a guinea, without saying a word about it; and then to you who
value time so much, and money so little, it will cut
the matter short. But come now (for I see you will
give nothing), I should be mighty glad to know what
is the sort of good you do yourselves, since you always object to what is done by others. "Sir," said

Mr. Fantom, " the object of a true philosopher is to diffuse light and knowledge. I wish to see the whole world enlightened."

Trueman. Amen! if you mean with the light of the gospel. But if you mean that one religion is as good as another, and that no religion is best of all; and that we shall become wiser and better by setting aside the very means which Providence bestowed to make us wise and good : in short, if you want to make the whole world philosophers, why they had better stay as they are. But as to the true light, I wish it to reach the very lowest, and I therefore bless God for charity-schools, as instruments of diffusing it among the poor.

Fantom, who had no reason to expect that his friend was going to call upon him for a subscription on this account, ventured to praise them, saying : " I am no enemy to these institutions. I would indeed change the object of instruction, but I would have the whole world instructed."

Here Mrs. Fantom, who, with her daughter, had quietly sat by at their work, ventured to put in a word, a liberty she seldom took with her husband ; who in his zeal to make the whole world free and happy, was too prudent to include his wife among the objects on whom he wished to confer freedom and happiness. " Then, my dear," said she, " I wonder you do not let your own servants be taught a little. The maids can scarcely tell a letter, or say the Lord's Prayer, and you know you will not allow them time to learn. William, too, has never been at church since we came out of town. He was at first very orderly and obedient, but now he is seldom sober of an evening ; and in the morning when he should be rubbing the tables in the parlor, he is generally lolling upon them, and reading your little manual of the new philosophy."—" Mrs. Fantom," said her husband, angrily, " you know that my labors for the public good leave me little time to think of my own family. I must have a great field, I like to de good to hundreds at once."

"I am very glad of that papa," said Miss Polly; "for then I hope you will not refuse to subscribe to all those pretty children at the Sunday-school, as you did yesterday, when the gentleman came a begging, because that is the very thing you were wishing for; there are two or three hundred to be done good at once."

Trueman. Well, Mr. Fantom, you are a wonderful man to keep up such a stock of benevolence at so small an expense. To love mankind so dearly, and yet avoid all opportunities of doing them good; to have such a noble zeal for the millions, and to feel so little compassion for the units; to long to free empires and enlighten kingdoms; and yet deny instruction to your own village, and comfort to your own family. Surely none but a philosopher could indulge so much philanthropy, and so much frugality at the same time. But come, do assist me in a petition I am making in our poorhouse; between the old, whom I want to have better fed, and the young, whom I want to have more worked.

Fantom. Sir, my mind is so engrossed with the partition of Poland, that I can not bring it down to an object of such insignificance. I despise the man whose benevolence is swallowed up in the narrow concerns of his own family, or parish, or country. .

Trueman. Well, now I have a notion that it is as well to do one's own duty, as the duty of another man; and that to do good at home, is as well as to do good abroad. For my part, I had as live help Tom Saunders to freedom as a Pole or a South American, though I should be very glad to help their too. But one must begin to love somewhere, and to do good somewhere; and I think it is as natural to love one's own family, and to do good in one's own neighborhood, as to anybody else. And if every man in every family, parish, and county, did the same,

why then all the schemes would meet, and the end
of one parish, where I was doing good, would be the
beginning of another parish where somebody else
was doing good; so my schemes would jut into my
neighbor's; his projects would unite with those of
some other local reformer; and all would fit with a
sort of dove-tail exactness. And what is better, all
would join in furnishing a living comment on that
practical precept: "Thou shalt love the Lord thy
God with all thy heart, and thy neighbor as thyself."

Fantom. Sir, a man of large views will be on the
watch for great occasions to prove his benevolence.

Trueman. Yes, sir; but if they are so distant that
he can not reach them, or so vast that he can not
grasp them, he may let a thousand little, snug, kind,
good actions, slip through his fingers in the mean-
while: and so between the great things, that he can
not do, and the little ones that he will not do, life
passes and nothing will be done.

Just at this moment Miss Polly Fantom (whose
mother had gone out some time before) started up,
let fall her work, and cried out, " O papa, do but look
what a monstrous great fire there is yonder on the
common! If it were the fifth of November, I should
think it were a bonfire. Look how it blazes!"—" I
see plain enough what it is," said Mr. Fantom, sitting
down again without the least emotion. "It is Jenkins's cottage on fire."—" What, poor John Jenkins,
who works in our garden, papa?" said the poor girl,
in great terror. "Do not be frightened, child," answered Fantom, "we are safe enough; the wind blows
the other way. Why did you disturb us for such a
trifle, as it was so distant? Come, Mr. Trueman.
sit down."—" Sit down," said Mr. Trueman, "I am
not a stock, sir, nor a stone, but a man; made of
the same common nature with Jenkins, whose house
is burning. Come along—let us fly and help him,"
continued he, running to the door in such haste that
he forgot to take his hat, though it hung just before

him—" Come Mr. Fantom—come, my little dear—I
wish your mamma was here—I am sorry she went
out just now—we may all do some good; everybody
may be of some use at a fire. Even you, Miss Polly,
may save some of these poor people's things in your
apron, while your papa and I hand the buckets." All
this he said as he run along with the young lady in
his hand; not doubting but Fantom and his whole
family were following close behind him. But the
present distress was neither grand enough nor far
enough from home to satisfy the wide-stretched benevolence of the philosopher, who sat down within
sight of the flames to work at a new pamphlet, which
now swallowed up his whole soul, on universal benevolence.

His daughter, indeed, who happily was not yet a
philosopher, with Mr. Trueman, followed by the
maids, reached the scene of distress. William Wilson, the footman, refused to assist, glad of such an
opportunity of being revenged on Jenkins, whom he
called a surly fellow, for presuming to complain, because William always purloined the best fruit for himself before he set it on his master's table. Jenkins
also, whose duty it was to be out of doors, had refused to leave his own work in the garden, to do
Will's work in the house while he got drunk, or read
the Rights of Man.

The little dwelling of Jenkins burnt very furiously.
Mr. Trueman's exertions were of the greatest service. He directed the willing, and gave an example
to the slothful. By living in London, he had been
more used to the calamity of fire than the country
people, and knew better what was to be done. In the
midst of the bustle he saw one woman only who
never attempted to be of the least use. She ran back-
ward and forward, wringing her hands, and crying
out in a tone of piercing agony, " Oh, my child! my
little Tommy! will no one save my Tommy?"—Any
woman might have uttered the same words, but the

look which explained them could only come from a mother. Trueman did not stay to ask if she were owner of the house, and mother of the child. It was his way to do all the good which could be done first, and then to ask questions. All he said was, "Tell me which is the room?" The poor woman, now speechless through terror, could only point up to a little window in the thatch, and then sunk on the ground.

Mr. Trueman made his way through a thick smoke, and ran up the narrow staircase which the fire had not reached. He got safely to the loft, snatched up the little creature, who was sweetly sleeping in its poor hammock, and brought him down naked in his arms; and as he gave him to the half-distracted mother, he felt that her joy and gratitude would have been no bad pay for the danger he had run, even if no higher motive had set him to work. Poor Jenkins, half stupified by his misfortune, had never thought of his child; and his wife, who expected every hour to make him father to a second, had not been able to do anything toward saving little Tommy.

Mr. Trueman now put the child into Miss Fantom's apron, saying, "Did I not tell you, my dear, that everybody could be of use at a fire?" He then desired her to carry the child home, and ordered the poor woman to follow her, saying, he would return himself as soon as he had seen all safe in the cottage.

When the fire was quite out, and Mr. Trueman could be of no further use, he went back to Mr. Fantom's. The instant he opened the parlor door, he eagerly cried out, "Where is the poor woman, Mr. Fantom?"—"Not in my house, I assure you," answered the philosopher. "Give me leave to tell you, it was a very romantic thing to send her and her child to me: you should have provided for them at once, like a prudent man."—"I thought I had done so," replied Trueman, "by sending them to the nearest and best house in the parish, as the poor woman

seemed to stand in need of immediate assistance."
"So immediate," said Fantom, "that I would not let
her come into my house, for fear of what might happen. So I packed her off, with her child in her arms,
to the workhouse, with orders to the overseers not to
let her want for anything."

"And what right have you, Mr. Fantom," cried
Trueman in a high tone. "to expect that the overseers
will be more humane than yourself? But is it possible you can have sent that helpless creature, not only
to walk, but to carry a naked child at such a time of
night, to a place so distant, so ill provided, and in such
a condition? I hope at least you have furnished them
with clothes, for all their own little stores were burnt."
"Not I, indeed," said Fantom. "What is the use
of parish officers, but to look after these petty things?"

It was Mr. Trueman's way, when he began to feel
very angry, not to allow himself to speak; "because,"
he used to say, "if I give vent to my feelings, I am
sure, by some hasty word, to cut myself out work for
repentance." So without making any answer, or
even changing his clothes, which were very wet and
dirty from having worked so hard at the fire, he
walked out again, having first inquired the road the
woman had taken. At the door he met Mrs. Fantom
returning from her visit. He told her his tale, which
she had no sooner heard, than she resolved to accom-
pany him in search of Jenkins's wife. She had a
wide common to walk over before she could reach
either the workhouse or the nearest cottage. She had
crawled along with her baby as far as she was able;
but having met with no refreshment at Mr. Fantom's,
and her strength quite failing her, she had sunk down
on the middle of the common. Happily, Mr. Trueman and Mrs. Fantom came up at this very time.
The former had had the precaution to bring a cordial.
and the latter had gone back and stuffed her pockets
with old baby-linen. Mr. Trueman soon procured
the assistance of a laborer, who happened to pass by.

to help him to carry the mother, and Mrs. Fantom carried the little shivering baby.

As soon as they were safely lodged, Mr. Trueman set off in search of poor Jenkins, who was distressed to know what was become of his wife and child; for having heard that they were seen going toward Mr. Fantom's, he despaired of any assistance from that quarter. Mr. Trueman felt no small satisfaction in uniting this poor man to his little family. There was something very moving in this meeting, and in the pious gratitude they expressed for their deliverance. They seemed to forget they had lost their all, in the joy they felt that they had not lost each other. And some disdainful great ones might have smiled to see so much rapture expressed at the safety of a child born to no inheritance but poverty. These are among the feelings with which Providence sometimes overpays the want of wealth. The good people also poured out prayers and blessings on their deliverer, who, not being a philosopher, was no more ashamed of praying with them than he had been of working for them. Mr. Trueman, while assisting at the fire, had heard that Jenkins and his wife were both very honest and very pious people; so he told them he would not only pay for their new lodgings, but undertook to raise a subscription among his friends at the Cat and Bagpipes toward rebuilding their cottage; and farther engaged, that if they would promise to bring up the child in the fear of God, he would stand godfather.

This exercise of Christian charity had given such a cheerful flow to Mr. Trueman's spirits, that long before he got home he had lost every trace of ill humor. "Well, Mr. Fantom," said he, gayly, as he opened the door, "now do tell me how you could possibly refuse going to help me to put out the fire at Mr Jenkins's?"—"Because," said Fantom, "I was engaged, sir, in a far nobler project than putting out a fire in a little thatched cottage. Sir, I was contriving to put out a fire too; a conflagration of a far more

dreadful kind—a fire, sir, in the extinction of which
universal man is concerned—I was contriving a scheme
to extinguish the fires of the inquisition."—" Why,
man, they don't blaze that I know of," retorted Trueman. " I own, that of all the abominable engines
which the devil ever invented to disgrace religion and
plague mankind, that. inquisition was the very worst.
But I do not believe popery has ventured at these
diabolical tricks since the earthquake at Lisbon; so
that a bucket of real water, carried to the real fire at
Jenkins's cottage, would have done more good than
a wild plan to put out an imaginary flame which no
longer burns. And let me tell you, sir, dreadful as
that evil was, God can send his judgments on other
sins besides superstition; so it behooves us to take
heed of the other extreme, or we may have our earth-
quakes too. The hand of God is not shortened, sir,
that it can not destroy, any more than it can not save.
In the meantime, I must repeat it, you and I are rather
called upon to serve a neighbor from perishing in the
flames of his house, just under our own window, than
to write about the fires of the inquisition, which, if fear,
or shame, or the restoration of common sense, had
not already put out, would have hardly received a
check from such poor hands as you and I."

" Sir," said Fantom, "Jenkins is an impertinent fellow; and I owe him a grudge, because he says he
had rather forfeit the favor of the best master in England than work in my garden on a Sunday. And
when I ordered him to read the Age of Reason, instead of going to church, he refused to work for me
at all, with some impertinent hint about God and
mammon.

" Oh, did he so?" said Mr. Trueman. " Now I
will stand godfather to his child, and make him a
handsome present into the bargain. Indeed, a man
must be a philosopher with a vengeance, if when he
sees a house on fire, he stays to consider whether the
owner has offended him. Oh, Mr. Fantom, I will

forgive you still, if you will produce me, out of all your philosophy, such a sentence as ' Love your enemy—do good to them that hate you—if thine enemy hunger, feed him; if he thirst, give him drink;' I will give up the blessed gospel for the Age of Reason, if you will only bring me one sentiment equivalent to this.''

Next day Mr. Trueman was obliged to go to London on business; but returned soon, as the time he had allotted to spend with Mr. Fantom was not yet elapsed. He came down the sooner, indeed, that he might bring a small sum of money which the gentlemen at the Cat and Bagpipes had cheerfully subscribed for Jenkins. Trueman did not forget to desire his wife to make up also a quantity of clothing for this poor family, to which he did not neglect to add a parcel of good books, which indeed always made a part of his charities, as he used to say there was something cruel in the kindness which was anxious to relieve the bodies of men, but was negligent of their souls. He stood in person to the new-born child, and observed with much pleasure, that Jenkins and his wife thought a christening, not a season for merry-making, but a solemn act of religion. And they dedicated their infant to his Maker with becoming seriousness.

Trueman left the cottage, and got back to Mr. Fantom's just as the family were going to sit down to dinner, as he had promised.

When they sat down, Mr. Fantom was not a little out of humor to see his table in some disorder. William was also rather more negligent than usual If the company called for bread, he gave them beer, and he took away the clean plates, and gave them dirty ones. Mr. Fantom soon discovered that his servant was very drunk: he flew into a violent passion, and ordered him out of the room, charging that he should not appear in his presence in that condition William obeyed; but having slept an hour or two,

and got about half sober, he again made his appearance. His master gave him a most severe reprimand,
and called him an idle, drunken, vicious fellow. "Sir,"
said William, very pertly, "if I do get drunk now and
then, I only do it for the good of my country, and in
obedience to your wishes." Mr. Fantom, thoroughly
provoked, now began to scold him in words not fit to
be repeated, and asked him what he meant. "Why,
sir," said William, "you are a philosopher, you know,
and I have often overheard you say to your company,
that private vices are public benefits; and so I thought
that getting drunk was as pleasant a way of doing
good to the public as any, especially when I could
oblige my master at the same time."

"Get out of my house," said Mr. Fantom, in a
great rage. "I do not desire to stay a moment longer," said William; "so pay me my wages."—"Not
I indeed," replied the master; "nor will I give you a
character; so never let me see your face again."
William took his master at his word, and not only
got out of the house, but went out of the country too
as fast as possible. When they found he was really
gone, they made a hue-and-cry, in order to detain him
till they examined if he had left everything in the
house as he had found it. But William had got out
of reach, knowing he could not stand such a scrutiny.
On examination, Mr. Fantom found that all his old
port was gone, and Mrs. Fantom missed three of her
best new spoons. William was pursued, but without
success; and Mr. Fantom was so much discomposed
that he could not for the rest of the day talk on any
subject but his wine and his spoons, nor harangue on
any project but that of recovering both by bringing
William to justice.

Some days passed away, in which Mr. Fantom,
having had time to cool, began to be ashamed that he
had been betrayed into such ungoverned passion. He
made the best excuse he could; said no man was perfect, and though he owned he had been too violent.

yet still he hoped William would be brought to the
punishment he deserved. "In the meantime," said
Mr Trueman, "seeing how ill philosophy has agreed
with your man, suppose you were to set about teaching your maids a little religion?" Mr. Fantom coolly
replied, that 'the impertinent retort of a drunken
footman could not spoil a system."—"Your system,
however, and your own behavior," said Trueman,
"have made that footman a scoundrel; and you are
answerable for his offences."—"Not I, truly," said
Fantom; "he has seen me do no harm; he has neither seen me cheat, gamble, nor get drunk; and I
defy you to say I corrupt my servants. I am a moral
man, sir."

"Mr. Fantom," said Trueman, "if you were to
get drunk every day, and game every night, you would,
indeed, endanger your own soul, and give a dreadful
example to your family; but great as those sins are,
and God forbid that I should attempt to lessen them!
still they are not worse, nay, they are not so bad as
the pestilent doctrines with which you infect your
house and your neighborhood. A bad action is like
a single murder. The consequence may end with
the crime, to all but the perpetrator; but a wicked
principle is throwing lighted gunpowder into a town;
it is poisoning a river; there are no bounds, no cer-
tainty, no ends to its mischief. The ill effects of the
worst action may cease in time, and the consequences
of your bad example may end with your life; but
souls may be brought to perdition by a wicked principle, after the author of it has been dead for ages."

Fantom. You talk like an ignoramus, who has
never read the new philosophy. All this nonsense
of future punishment is now done away. It is *our*
benevolence which makes us reject your creed; we
can no more believe in a deity who permits so much
evil in the present world, than one who threatens
eternal punishment in the next.

Trueman. What! shall mortal man be more mer-

ciful than God ?   Do you pretend to be more com·
passionate than that gracious Father who sent his
own Son into the world to die for sinners ?

Fantom. You take all your notions of the Deity
from the vulgar views your Bible gives you of him.
" To be sure I ω," said Trueman : " can you tell me
any way of getting a better notion of him ?   I do not
want any of your farthing-candle philosophy in the
broad sunshine of the Gospel, Mr. Fantom.   My
Bible tells me that 'God is love ;' not merely
loving, but LOVE.   Now do you think a Being, whose
very essence is love, would permit any misery among
his children here, if it was not to be, some way or
other, or some where or other, for their good?   You
forget too, that in a world where there is sin, there
must be misery.   Then, too, I suppose, God permits
this very misery partly to exercise the sufferers and
partly to try the prosperous ; for by trouble God
corrects some and tries others.   Suppose now, Tom
Saunders had not been put in prison, you and I——
no, I beg pardon, *you* saved your guinea ; well then,
our club and I could not have shown our kindness in getting him out ; nor would poor Saunders
himself have had an opportunity of exercising his
own patience and submission under want and imprisonment.   So you see one reason why God permits
misery, is that good men may have an opportunity of
lessening it."   Mr. Fantom replied, " There is no
object which I have more at heart ; I have, as I told
you, a plan in my head of such universal benevolence
as to include the happiness of all mankind."—" Mr.
Fantom," said Trueman, " I feel that I have a general
good will to all my brethren of mankind ; and if I
had as much money in my purse as I have love in my
heart, I trust I should prove it : all I say is, that, in a
station of life where I can not do much, I am more
called upon to procure the happiness of a poor neigh
bor, who has no one else to look to, than to form wild
plans for the good of mankind, too extensive to be

accomplished, and too chimerical to be put in prac
tice.   It is the height of folly for a little ignorant
tradesman to distract himself with projecting schemes
which require the wisdom of scholars, the experience
of statesmen, and the power of kings to accomplish.
I can not free whole countries, nor reform the evils
of society at large, but I *can* free an aggrieved wretch
in a workhouse ; I *can* relieve the distresses of one
of my journeymen; and I *can* labor to reform myself
and my own family."

Some weeks after this a letter was brought to Mr.
Fantom from his late servant William. who had been
turned away for drunkenness, as related above, and
who had also robbed his master of some wine and
some spoons.   Mr. Fantom, glancing his eye over
the letter, said, " It is dated from Chelmsford jail;
that rascal has got into prison.   I am glad of it, with
all my heart; it is the fittest place for such scoundrels.
I hope he will be sent to Botany Bay, if not hanged."
" O, ho! my good friend," said Trueman, " then I
find that in abolishing all prisons you would just let
one stand for the accommodation of those who would
happen to rob *you*.   General benevolence, I see, is
compatible with particular resentments, though individual kindness is not consistent with universal philanthropy."   Mr. Fantom drily observed, that he was
not fond of jokes, and proceeded to read the letter.
It expressed an earnest wish that his late master
would condescend to pay him one visit in his dark
and doleful abode; as he wished to say a few words
to him before the dreadful sentence of the law, which
had already been pronounced, should be executed.

" Let us go and see the poor fellow," said Trueman ; " it is but a morning's ride.   If he is really so
near his end it would be cruel to refuse him."   " Not
I, truly," said Fantom ; " he deserves nothing at my
hands but the halter he is likely to meet with.   Such
port is not to be had for money! and the spoons, part
of my new dozen !"—" As to the wine," said True

6

man, " I am afraid you must give that up, but the
only way to get any tidings of the spoons is to go
and hear what he has to say ; I have no doubt but he
will make such a confession as may be very useful to
others, which, you know, is one grand advantage of
punishments ; and, besides, we may afford him some
little comfort." " As to comfort he deserves none
from me," said Fantom ; " and as to his confessions,
they can be of no use to me, but as they give me a
chance of getting my spoons ; so I do not much care
if I do take a ride with you."

When they came to the prison, Mr. Trueman's
tender heart sunk within him. He deplored the corrupt nature of man, which makes such rigorous
confinement indispensably needful, not merely for the
punishment of the offender, but for the safety of society. Fantom, from mere trick and habit, was just
preparing a speech on benevolence. and the cruelty
of imprisonment ; for he had a set of sentiments collected from the new philosophy which he always
kept by him. The naming a man in power brought
out the ready cut and dried phrase, against oppression. The idea of rank included every vice, that of
poverty every virtue ; and he was furnished with all
the incentives against the cruelty of laws, punishments, and prisons, which the new lexicon has produced. But his mechanical benevolence was suddenly checked ; the recollection of his old port and
his new spoons cooled his ardor, and he went on
without saying a word.

When they reached the cell where the unhappy
William was confined, they stopped at the door
The poor wretch had thrown himself on the ground,
as well as his chains would permit. He groaned pit-
eously ; and was so swallowed up with a sense of
his own miseries, that he neither heard the door
open, nor saw the gentlemen. He was attempting
to pray, but in an agony which made his words hardly
intelligible. Thus much they could make out—" God

be merciful to me a sinner, the chief of sinners!"
then, suddenly attempting to start up, but prevented
by his irons, he roared out, "O God! thou canst *not*
be merciful to me, for I have denied thee; I have
ridiculed my Savior who died for me; I have broken
his laws; I have derided his word; I have resisted
his Spirit; I have laughed at that heaven which is
shut against me; I have denied the truth of those
torments which await me. To-morrow! to-morrow!
O for a longer space for repentance! O for a short
reprieve from hell!"

Mr. Trueman wept so loud that it drew the attention of the criminal, who now lifted up his eyes, and
cast on his late master a look so dreadful that Fantom
wished for a moment that he had given up all hope
of the spoons, rather than have exposed himself to
such a scene. At length the poor wretch said, in a
low voice that would have melted a heart of stone,
"O, sir, are you there? I did indeed wish to see
you before my dreadful sentence is put in execution.
Oh, sir! to-morrow! to-morrow! But I have a confession to make to you." This revived Mr. Fantom,
who again ventured to glance a hope at the spoons
"Sir," said William, "I could not die without making my confession." "Ay, and restitution too, I
hope," replied Fantom: "where are my spoons?"
"Sir, they are gone with the rest of my wretched
booty. But oh, sir! those spoons make so petty an
article in my black account, that I hardly think of
them. Murder! sir, murder is the crime for which
I am justly doomed to die. Oh, sir, who can abide
the anger of an offended God? Who can dwell
with everlasting burnings?" As this was a question
which even a philosopher could not answer, Mr. Fantom was going to steal off, especially as he now gave
up all hope of the spoons; but William called him
back: "Stay, sir, stay, I conjure you, as you will
answer it at the bar of God. You must hear the sins
of which you have been the occasion. You are the

cause of my being about to suffer a shameful death.
Yes, sir, you made me a drunkard, a thief, and a mur-
derer." "How dare you, William," cried Mr. Fantom, with great emotion, "accuse me with being the
cause of such horrid crimes?" "Sir," answered the
criminal, "from you I learned the principles which
lead to those crimes. By the grace of God I should
never have fallen into sins deserving of the gallows,
if I had not overheard you say there was no hereafter,
no judgment, no future reckoning. O, sir! there is
a hell, dreadful, inconceivable, eternal!" Here,
through the excess of anguish, the poor fellow fainted away. Mr. Fantom, who did not at all relish this
scene, said to his friend, "Well, sir, we will go, if
you please, for you see there is nothing to be done."

"Sir," replied Mr. Trueman, mournfully, "you
may go if you please, but I shall stay, for I see there
is a great deal to be done."—"What!" rejoined the
other, "do you think it is possible his life can be
saved." "No, indeed," said Trueman; "but I hope
it possible his soul may be saved." "I do not understand these things," said Fantom, making toward the
door. "Nor I neither," said Trueman: "but as a
fellow-sinner, I am bound to do what I can for this
poor man. Do you go home, Mr. Fantom and finish
your treatise on universal benevolence, and the blessed effects of philosophy; and hark ye, be sure you
let the frontispiece of your book represent *William
on the gibbet;* that will be what our minister calls a
PRACTICAL ILLUSTRATION. You know I hate theories: this is *realizing;* this is PHILOSOPHY made
easy to the meanest capacity. This is the precious
fruit which grows on that darling tree, so many slips
of which have been transplanted from that land of
liberty of which it is the native, but which, with all
your digging, planting, watering, dunging, and dressing, will, I trust, never thrive in this blessed land of
ours."

Mr. Fantom sneaked off to finish his work at home;
and Mr. Trueman stayed to finish his in the prison

He passed the night with the wretched convict; he prayed with him and for him, and read to him the penitential psalms, and some portion of the gospel. But he was too humble and too prudent a man to venture out of his depth by arguments and consolations which he was not warranted to use : this he left for the clergyman—but he pressed on William the great duty of making the only amends now in his power, to those whom he had led astray. They then drew up the following paper, which Mr. Trueman got printed, and gave away at the place of execution.

' *The last words, confession, and dying speech of* WILLIAM WILSON, *who was executed at Chelmsford for murder.*

" I was bred up in the fear of God, and lived with credit in many sober families, in which I was a faithful servant ; but being tempted by a little higher wages, I left a good place to go and live with Mr. Fantom, who, however, made good none of his fine promises, but proved a hard master. Full of fine words and charitable speeches in favor of the poor; but apt to oppress, overwork, and underpay them. In his service I was not allowed time to go to church. This troubled me at first, till I overheard my master say, that going to church was a superstitious prejudice, and only meant for the vulgar. Upon this I resolved to go no more ; for I thought there could not be two religions, one for the master, and one for the servant. Finding my master never prayed, I too left off praying : this gave Satan great power over me, so that I from that time fell into almost every sin. I was very uneasy at first, and my conscience gave me no rest ; but I was soon reconciled by overhearing my master and another gentleman say, that death was only an eternal sleep, and hell and judgment were but an invention of priests to keep the poor in order. I mention this as a warning to all masters and mistresses to take care what they converse about while servants are waiting at table. They can not tell how many souls they have sent to perdition by such loose talk. The crime for which I die is the natural consequence of the principles I learned of my master. A rich man, indeed, who throws off religion, may escape the gallows, because want does not drive him to commit those crimes which lead to it; but what shall restrain a needy man, who has been taught that there is no dreadful reckoning? Honesty is but a dream without the awful sanctions of heaven and hell. Virtue is but a shadow, if it be stripped of the terrors and the promises of the gospel. Morality is but an empty name, if it be destitute of the principle and power of Christianity. Oh, my dear fellow-servants! take warning by my sad fate; never be tempted away from a sober service for the sake of a little more wages: never venture your immortal souls in houses where God is not feared. And now hear me, O, my God, though I have blasphemed thee! forgive me, O my Savior, though I have denied thee! Oh Lord most holy, O God most mighty, deliver me from the bitter pains of eternal death, and receive my soul for His sake who died for sinners. " WILLIAM WILSON."

Mr. Trueman would never leave this poor penitent till he was launched into eternity, but attended him with the minister in the cart. This pious clergyman never cared to say what he thought of William's state. When Mr. Trueman ventured to mention his hope, that though his penitence was late, yet it was sincere, and spoke of the dying thief on the cross as a ground of encouragement, the minister with a very serious look, made this answer: "Sir, that instance is too often brought forward on occasions to which it does not apply : I do not choose to say anything to your application of it in the present case, but I will answer you in the words of a good man speaking of the penitent thief: ' There is *one* such instance given that nobody might despair, and there is *but* one, that nobody might presume.'"

III. THE TWO SHOEMAKERS.

JACK BROWN and JAMES STOCK were two lads apprenticed to Mr. Williams, a shoemaker, in a small town in Oxfordshire. They were near the same age, but of very different characters and dispositions.

Brown was eldest son to a farmer in good circumstances, who gave the usual apprentice fee with him. Being a wild, giddy boy, whom his father could not well manage or instruct in farming, he thought it better to send him out to learn a trade at a distance than to let him idle about at home, for Jack always preferred bird's-nesting and marbles to any other employment; he would trifle away the day, when his father thought he was at school, with any boys he could meet with, who were as idle as himself; and he could never be prevailed upon to do, or to learn anything, while a game at taw could be had for love or money. All this time his little brothers, much younger than himself, were beginning to follow the plough, or to carry the corn to the mill as soon as they were able to mount a cart-horse.

Jack, however, who was a lively boy, and did not naturally want either sense or good-nature, might have turned out well enough if he had not had the misfortune to be his mother's favorite. She concealed and forgave all his faults. To be sure he was a little wild, she would say, but he would not make the worse man for that, for Jack had a good spirit of his own, and she would not have it broke, and so make

a mope of the boy. The farmer, for a quiet life, as
it is called, gave up all these points to his wife, and,
with them, gave up the future virtue and happiness
of his child. He was a laborious and industrious
man, but had no religion; he thought only of the
gains and advantages of the present day, and never
took the future into the account. His wife managed
him entirely, and as she was really notable he did
not trouble his head about anything farther. If she
had been careless in her dairy, he would have storm-
ed and sworn; but as she only ruined one child by
indulgence, and almost broke the hearts of the rest
by unkindness, he gave himself little concern about
the matter. The cheese, certainly, was good, and
that, indeed, is a great point; but she was neglectful
of her children and a tyrant to her servants. Her
husband's substance, indeed, was not wasted, but his
happiness was not consulted. His house, it is true,
was not dirty, but it was the abode of fury, ill-tem-
per, and covetousness. And the farmer, though he
did not care for liquor, was too often driven to the
public-house in the evening because his own was
neither quiet nor comfortable. The mother was always scolding, and the children were always crying.

Jack, however, notwithstanding his idleness, picked
up a little reading and writing, but never would learn
to cast an account—that was too much labor. His
mother was desirous he should continue at school,
not so much for the sake of his learning, which she
had not sense enough to value, but to save her darling
from the fatigue of labor, for if he had not gone to
school she knew he must have gone to work, and she
thought the former was the least tiresome of the two.
Indeed this foolish woman had such an opinion of
his genius, that she used from a child to think he
was too wise for anything but a parson, and hoped
she should live to see him one. She did not wish
to see her son a minister because she loved either
.earning or piety, but because she thought it would

make Jack a gentleman, and set him above his brothers.

Farmer Brown still hoped, that though Jack was likely to make but an idle and ignorant farmer, yet he might make no bad tradesman, when he should be removed from the indulgences of a father's house, and from a silly mother, whose fondness kept him back in everything. This woman was enraged when she found that so fine a scholar as she took Jack to be, was to be put apprentice to a shoemaker. The farmer, however, for the first time in his life, would have his own way. But being a worldly man, and too apt to mind only what is falsely called *the main chance*, instead of being careful to look out for a sober, prudent, and religious master for his son, he left all that to accident, as if it had been a thing of little or no consequence. This is a very common fault, and fathers who are guilty of it are in a great measure answerable for the future sins and errors of their children, when they come out into the world and set up for themselves. If a man gives his son a good education, a good example, and a good master, it is indeed *possible* that the son may not turn out well, but it does not often happen, and when it does, the father has no blame resting on him; and it is a great point toward a man's comfort to have his conscience quiet in that respect, however God may think fit to overrule events.

The farmer, however, took care to desire his friends to inquire for a shoemaker who had good business, and was a good workman; and the mother did not forget to put in her word, and desired that it might be one who was not *too strict*, for Jack had been brought up tenderly, was a meek boy, and could not bear to be contradicted in anything. This is the common notion of meekness among people who do not take up their notions on rational and Christian grounds.

Mr. Williams was recommended to the farmer as

being the best shoemaker in the town in which he lived, and not a strict master. So without farther inquiries to Mr. Williams he went.

James Stock, who was the son of an honest laborer in the next village, was bound out by the parish in consideration of his father having so numerous a family that he was not able to put him out himself. James was in everything the very reverse of his new companion. He was a modest, industrious, pious youth, and though so poor, and the child of a laborer, was a much better scholar than Jack, who was a wealthy farmer's son. His father had, it is true, been able to give him but very little schooling, for he was obliged to be put to work when quite a child. When very young he used to run of errands for Mr. Thomas, the curate of the parish, a very kind-hearted young gentleman, who boarded next door to his father's cottage. He used also to rub down and saddle his horse, and do any other little job for him in the most civil, obliging manner. All this so recommended him to the clergyman, that he would often send for him of an evening, after he had done his day's work in the field, and condescended to teach him himself to write and cast accounts, as well as to instruct him in the principles of his religion. It was not merely out of kindness for the little good-natured services James did him, that he showed him this favor, but also for his readiness in the catechism, and his devout behavior at church.

The first thing that drew the minister's attention to this boy, was the following: He had frequently given him half-pence and pence for holding his horse and carrying him to water before he was big enough to be further useful to him. On Christmas day he was surprised to see James at church, reading out of a handsome new prayer-book; he wondered how he came by it, for he knew there was nobody in the parish likely to have given it to him, for at that time there were no Sunday-schools, and the father could not afford it, he was sure.

"Well, James," said he, as he saw him when they came out, "you made a good figure at church to-day; it made you look like a man and a Christian, not only to have so handsome a book, but to be so ready in all parts of the service. How came you by that book?" James owned modestly, that he had been a whole year saving up the money by single half-pence, all of which had been of the minister's own giving, and that in all that time he had not spent a single farthing on his own diversions. "My dear boy," said the good Mr. Thomas, "I am much mis-taken if·thou dost not turn out well in the world, for two reasons: first, from thy saving turn and self-de-nying temper, and next, because thou didst devote the first eighteen-pence thou wast ever worth in the world to so good a purpose."

James bowed and blushed, and from that time Mr. Thomas began to take more notice of him, and to in-struct him as I said above. As James soon grew able to do him more considerable service, he would now and then give him a sixpence. This he constantly saved till it became a little sum, with which he bought shoes and stockings, well knowing that his poor father, with a large family and low wages, could not buy them for him. As to what little money he earned himself by his daily labor in the field, he constantly carried it to his mother every Saturday night, to buy bread for the family, which was a pretty help to them.

As James was not over-stout in his make, his father thankfully accepted the offer of the parish-officers to bind out his son to a trade. This good man, how-ever, had not, like Farmer Brown, the liberty of choosing a master for his son, or he would carefully have inquired if he was a proper man to have the care of youth; but Williams, the shoemaker, was already fixed on by those who were to put the boy

out, who told him if he wanted a master it must be
him or none, for the overseers had a better opinion of
Williams than he deserved, and thought it would be
the making of the boy to go to him. The father
knew that beggars must not be choosers, so he fitted
out James for his new place, having indeed little to
give him besides his blessing.

The worthy Mr. Thomas, however, kindly gave
him an old coat and waistcoat, which his mother,
who was a neat and notable woman, contrived to
make up for him herself, and when it was turned and
made fit for his size, it made him a very handsome
suit for Sundays, and lasted him a couple of years.

Here let me remark what a pity it is, that poor
women so seldom are able or willing to do these little
handy jobs themselves, and that they do not oftener
bring up their daughters to be more useful in family
work. They are great losers by it every way, not
only as they are disqualifying their girls from making
good wives hereafter, but they are losers in point of
present advantage, for gentry could much oftener afford to give a poor boy a jacket or a waistcoat, if it
was not for the expense of making it, which adds
very much to the cost. Many poor women would
often get an old coat, or a bit of coarse new cloth
given to them to fit out a boy, if the mothers or sis-
ters were known to be able to cut out to advantage,
and to make it up decently themselves.

The two young shoemakers were both settled at
Mr. Williams's, who, as he was known to be a good
workman, had plenty of business; he had sometimes
two or three journeymen, but no apprentices but
Jack and James.

Jack, who, with all his faults, was a keen, smart
boy, took to learn the trade quick enough, but the
difficulty was to make him stick two hours together
to his work. At every noise he heard in the street
down went the work--the last one way, the upper
leather another; the sole dropped on the ground,

and the thread dragged after him all the way up the
street. If a blind fiddler, a ballad-singer, a mountebank, a dancing bear, or a drum, were heard at a distance—out ran Jack—nothing could stop him, and
not a stitch more could he be prevailed on to do that
day. Every duty, every promise was forgotten for
the present pleasure—he could not resist the smallest
temptation—he never stopped for a moment to consider whether a thing was right or wrong, but whether he liked or disliked it. And as his ill-judging
mother took care to send him privately a good supply
of pocket-money, that deadly bane to all youthful
virtue, he had generally a few pence ready to spend,
and to indulge in the present diversion, whatever it
was. And what was still worse even than spending
his money, he spent his time, too, or rather his master's time Of this he was continually reminded by
James, to whom he always answered, "What have
you to complain about? It is nothing to you or any
one else; I spend nobody's money but my own."
"That may be," replied the other, "but you can not
say that it is your own time that you spend." He
insisted upon it that it was; but James fetched down
their indentures, and there showed him that he had
solemnly bound himself by that instrument not to
waste his master's property. "Now," quoth James,
"thy own time is a very valuable part of thy master's property." To this he replied, that "every one's
time was his own, and he should not sit moping all
day over his last—for his part, he thanked God he
was no parish 'prentice."

James did not resent this piece of silly impertinence,
as some silly lads would have done, nor fly out into
a violent passion; for even at this early age he had
begun to learn of Him *who was meek and lowly of
heart ;* and therefore, *when he was reviled, he reviled
not again.* On the contrary, he was so very kind and
gentle, that even Jack, vain and idle as he was, could

7

not help loving him, though he took care never to fol
low his advice.

Jack's fondness for his boyish and silly diversions
in the street, soon produced the effects which might
naturally be expected; and the same idleness which
led him to fly out into the town at the sound of a fiddle or the sight of a puppet-show, soon led him to
those places to which all these fiddles and shows
naturally lead—I mean the *alehouse*.   The acquaintance picked up in the street was carried on at the
Grayhound; and the idle pastimes of the boy soon
led to the destructive vices of the man.

As he was not an ill-tempered youth, nor naturally
much given to drink, a sober and prudent master, who
had been steady in his management and regular in his
own conduct, who would have recommended good
advice by a good example, might have made something of Jack.   But Mr. Williams, though a good
workman, and not a very hard or severe master, was
neither a sober nor a steady man : so far from it, that
he spent much more time at the Grayhound than at
home.   There was no order either in his shop or
family.   He left the chief care of his business to his
two young apprentices; and being but a worldly man,
he was at first disposed to show favor to Jack, much
more than to James, because he had more money,
and his father was better in the world than the father
of poor James.

At first, therefore, he was disposed to consider
James as a sort of drudge, who was to do all the me-
nial work of the family, and he did not care how little
he taught him of his trade.   With Mrs. Williams the
matter was still worse; she constantly called him
away from the business of his trade to wash the house,
nurse the child, turn the spit, or run of errands.   Here
I must remark, that though parish apprentices are
bound in duty to be submissive to both master and
mistress, and always to make themselves as useful as
they can in a family, and to be civil and humble, yet

it is the duty of masters always to remember, that if they are paid for instructing them in their trade, they ought conscientiously to instruct them in it, and not to employ them the greater part of their time in such household or other drudgery, as to deprive them of the opportunity of acquiring their trade. This practice is not the less unjust because it is common.

Mr. Williams soon found out that his favorite Jack would be of little use to him in the shop: for though he worked well enough, he did not care how little he did. Nor could he be of the least use to his master in keeping an account, or writing out a bill upon occasion; for, as he never could be made to learn to cipher, he did not know addition from multiplication.

One day one of the customers called at the shop in a great hurry, and desired his bill might be made out that minute. Mr. Williams, having taken a cup too much, made several attempts to put down a clear account, but the more he tried, the less he found himself able to do it. James, who was sitting at his last, rose up, and with great modesty, asked his master if he would please to give him leave to make out the bill, saying, that though but a poor scholar, he would do his best, rather than keep the gentleman waiting. Williams gladly accepted his offer, and confused as his head was with liquor, he yet was able to observe with what neatness, despatch, and exactness, the account was drawn out. From that time he no longer considered James as a drudge, but as one fitted for the high departments of the trade, and he was now regularly employed to manage the accounts, with which all the customers were so well pleased, that it contributed greatly to raise him in his master's esteem; for there were now never any of those blunders or false charges for which the shop had before been so famous.

James went on in a regular course of industry, and soon became the best workman Mr. Williams had ; but there many things in the family which he greatly

disapproved. Some of the journeymen used to swear,
drink, and sing licentious songs. All these things
were a great grief to his sober mind. He complained
to his master, who only laughed at him; and, indeed, as Williams did the same himself, he put it
out of his power to correct his servants, if he had
been so disposed. James, however, used always to
reprove them with great mildness indeed, but with
great seriousness also. This, but still more his own
excellent example, produced at length very good effects on such of the men as were not quite hardened
in sin.

What grieved him most, was the manner in which
the Sunday was spent. The master lay in bed all the
morning; nor did the mother or her children ever go
to church, except there was some new finery to be
shown, or a christening to be attended. The town's
people were coming to the shop all the morning, for
work which should have been sent home the night
before, had not the master been at the alehouse. And
what wounded James to the very soul was, that the
master expected the two apprentices to carry home
shoes to the country customers on the Sunday morning, which he wickedly thought was a saving of time,
as it prevented their hindering their work on the Saturday. These shameful practices greatly afflicted
poor James. He begged his master, with tears in his
eyes, to excuse him, but he only laughed at his
squeamish conscience, as he called it.

Jack did not dislike this part of the business, and
generally after he had delivered his parcel, wasted
good part of the day in nutting, playing at fives, or
dropping in at the public house: anything was better
to Jack than going to church.

James, on the other hand, when he was compelled
sorely against his conscience to carry home any goods
on a Sunday morning, always got up as soon as it
was light, knelt down and prayed heartily to God to
forgive him a sin which it was not in his power to

avoid. He took care not to lose a moment by the way; but as he was taking his walk with the utmost speed, to leave his shoes with the customers, he spent his time in endeavoring to keep up good thoughts in his mind, and praying that the day might come when his conscience might be delivered from this grievous burden. He was now particularly thankful that Mr. Thomas had formerly taught him so many psalms and chapters, which he used to repeat in these walks with great devotion.

He always got home before the rest of the family were up, dressed himself very clean, and went twice to church, as he greatly disliked the company and practices of his master's house, particularly on the sabbath-day, he preferred spending his evening alone, reading his Bible, which I had forgot to say the wor thy clergyman had given him when he left his native village. Sunday evening, which is to some people such a burden, was to James the highest holyday. He had formerly learnt a little how to sing a psalm of the clerk of his own parish, and this was now become a very delightful part of his evening exercise. And as Will Simpson, one of the journeymen, by James's advice and example, was now beginning to be of a more serious way of thinking, he often asked him to sit an hour with him, when they read the Bible, and talked it over together in a manner very pleasant and improving; and as Will was a famous singer, a psalm or two sung together was a very innocent pleasure.

James's good manners and civility to the customers drew much business to the shop; and his skill as a workman was so great, that every one desired that his shoes might be made by James. Williams grew so very idle and negligent, that he now totally neglected his affairs, and to hard drinking added deep gaming. All James's care, both of the shop and the accounts, could not keep things in any tolerable order. He represented to his master that they were growing worse and worse, and exhorted him, if he valued his credit as a tradesman, his comfort as a husband and father, his character as a master, and his soul as a Christian, to turn over a new leaf. Williams swore a great oath, that he would not be restrained in his pleasures to please a canting parish 'prentice, nor to humor a parcel of squalling brats; that let people say what they would of him, they should never say he was a *hypocrite*, and as long as they could not call him that, he did not care what else they called him.

In a violent passion he immediately went to the Grayhound, where he now spent not only every evening, which he had long done, but good part of the day and night also. His wife was very dressy, extravagant, and fond of company, and wasted at home as fast as her husband spent abroad, so that all the neighbors said, if it had not been for James, his master must have been a bankrupt long ago, but they were sure he could not hold it much longer.

As Jack Brown sung a good song, and played many diverting tricks, Williams liked his company, and often allowed him to make one at the Grayhound, where he would laugh heartily at his stories; so that every one thought Jack was the greater favorite—so he was as a companion in frolic, and foolery, and *pleasure*, as it is called; but he would not trust him with an inch of leather or sixpence in money: no, no —when business was to be done, or trust was to be reposed, James was the man: the idle and the drunken never trust one another, if they have common sense. They like to laugh, and sing, and riot, and drink together, but when they want a friend, a counsellor, a helper in business or in trouble, they go farther afield; and Williams, while he would drink with Jack, would trust James with untold gold; and even was foolishly tempted to neglect his business the more, from knowing that he had one at home who was taking care of it.

In spite of all James's care and diligence, however, things were growing worse and worse; the more

James saved, the more his master and mistress spent. One morning, just as the shop was opened, and James had set everybody to their respective work, and he himself was settling the business for the day, he found that his master was not yet come from the Grayhound. As this was now become a common case, he only grieved but did not wonder at it. While he was indulging sad thoughts on what would be the end of all this, in ran the tapster from the Grayhound, out of breath, and with a look of terror and dismay desired James would step over to the public house with him that moment, for that his master wanted him.

James went immediately, surprised at this unusual message. When he got into the kitchen of the public house, which he now entered for the first time in his life, though it was just opposite to the house in which he lived, he was shocked at the beastly disgusting appearance of everything he beheld. There was a table covered with tankards, punch-bowls, broken glasses, pipes, and dirty, greasy packs of cards, and all over wet with liquor; the floor was strewed with broken earthen cups, odd cards, and an EO table which had been shivered to pieces in a quarrel; behind the table stood a crowd of dirty fellows, with matted locks, hollow eyes, and faces smeared with tobacco. James made his way after the tapster, through this wretched-looking crew, to a settle which stood in the chimney corner. Not a word was uttered, but the silent horror seemed to denote something more than a mere common drunken bout.

What was the dismay of James when he saw his miserable master stretched out on the settle, in all the agonies of death! He had fallen into a fit, after having drank hard best part of the night, and seemed to have but a few minutes to live. In his frightful countenance was displayed the dreadful picture of sin and death, for he struggled at once under the guilt of intoxication and the pangs of a dying man. He recovered his senses for a few moments, and call-

ed out to ask if his faithful servant was come. James
went up to him, took him by his cold hand, but was
too much moved to speak. "Oh! James, James,"
cried he, in a broken voice, "pray for me, comfort
me." James spoke kindly to him, but was too honest to give him false comfort, as is too often done by
mistaken friends in these dreadful moments.

"James," said he, "I have been a bad master to
you; you would have saved me, soul and body, but
I would not let you; I have ruined my wife, my
children, and my own soul. Take warning, oh, take
warning by my miserable end," said he to his stupified companions; but none were able to attend to him
but James, who bid him lift up his heart to God, and
prayed heartily for him himself. "Oh!" said the
dying man, "it is too late, too late for me—but you
have still time," said he to the half drunken, terrified
crew around him. "Where is Jack?" Jack Brown
came forward, but was too much frightened to speak.
"O wretched boy!" said he, "I fear I shall have the
ruin of thy soul as well as my own to answer for.
Stop short. Take warning, now in the days of thy
youth. O James, James, thou dost not pray for me.
Death is dreadful to the wicked. O the sting of death
to a guilty conscience!" Here he lifted up his
ghastly eyes in speechless horror, grasped hard at
the hand of James, gave a deep, hollow groan, and
closed his eyes, never to open them but in an awful
eternity.

This was death in all its horrors! The gay companions of his sinful pleasures could not stand the
sight : all slank away like guilty thieves from their
late favorite friend ; no one was left to assist him but
his two apprentices. Brown was not so hardened
but that he shed many tears for his unhappy master,
and even made some hasty resolutions of amendment,
which were too soon forgotten.

While Brown stepped home to call the workmen
to come and assist in removing their poor master,

James stayed alone with the corpse, and employed those awful moments in indulging the most serious thoughts, and praying heartily to God that so terrible a lesson might not be thrown away upon him, but that he might be enabled to live in a constant state of preparation for death. The resolutions he made at this moment, as they were not made in his own strength, but in an humble reliance on God's gracious help, were of use to him as long as he lived, and if ever he was for a moment tempted to say or do a wrong thing, the remembrance of his poor dying master's last agonies, and the dreadful words he uttered, always operated as an instant check upon him.

When Williams was buried, and his affairs came to be inquired into, they were found to be in a sad condition. His wife, indeed, was the less to be pitied, as she had contributed her full share to the common ruin. James, however, did pity her, and by his skill in accounts, his known honesty, and the trust the creditors put in his word, things came to be settled rather better than Mrs. Williams expected.

Both Brown and James were now within a month or two of being out of their time. The creditors, as was said before, employed James to settle his late master's accounts, which he did in a manner so creditable to his abilities and his honesty, that they proposed to him to take the shop himself. He assured them it was utterly out of his power for want of money. As the creditors had not the least fear of being repaid, if it should please God to spare his life, they generously agreed among themselves to advance him a small sum of money without any security but his bond; for this he was to pay a very reasonable interest, and to return the whole in a given number of years. James shed tears of gratitude at this testimony to his character, and could hardly be prevailed on to accept their kindness, so great was his dread of being in debt.

He took the remainder of the lease from his mis
tress, and in settling affairs with her, took care to
make everything as advantageous to her as possible.
He never once allowed himself to think how unkind
she had been to him; he only saw in her the needy
widow of his deceased master, and the distressed
mother of an infant family, and was heartily sorry it
was not in his power to contribute to their support;
it was not only James's duty, but his delight, to return good for evil, for he was a Christian.

James Stock was now, by the blessing of God on
his own earnest endeavors, master of a considerable
shop, and was respected by the whole town for his
prudence, honesty, and piety.   Other apprentices
will do well to follow so praiseworthy an example,
and to remember, that the respectable master of a
large shop, and of a profitable business, was raised to
that creditable situation without money, friends, or
connexions, from the low beginning of a parish apprentice, by sobriety, industry, the fear of God, and
an obedience to the divine principles of the Christian
religion.

The Apprentice turned Master.

This sudden prosperity was a time of trial for
James, for we hardly know what we are ourselves till
we become our own masters.   There is, indeed, always a reasonable hope that a good servant will not
make a bad master, and that a faithful apprentice will
prove an honest tradesman.   But the heart of man is
deceitful, and some folks who seem to behave very
well while they are under subjection, no sooner get
a little power than their heads are turned, and they
grow prouder than those who are gentlemen born.
They forget at once that they were lately poor and
dependant themselves, so that one would think that
with their poverty they had lost their memory too.
I have known some who had suffered most hardships
in their early days, become the most hard and op-

pressive in their turn, so that they seem to forget
that fine considerate reason which God gives to the
children of Israel why they should be merciful to
their servants, *remembering*, said he, *that thou thyself
was a bondman.*

Young Mr. Stock did not so forget himself. He
had, indeed, the only sure guard from falling into
this error. It was not from any uneasiness in his
natural disposition, for that only just serves to make
folks good-natured when they are pleased, and patient
when they have nothing to vex them. James went
upon higher ground. He brought his religion into
all his actions; he did not give way to abusive language because he knew it was a sin. He did not
use his apprentices ill because he knew he had himself a Master in heaven.

He knew he owed his present happy situation to
the kindness of the creditors. But did he grow easy
and careless because he knew he had such friends?
No indeed. He worked with double diligence in
order to get out of debt, and to let these friends see
he did not abuse their kindness. Such behavior as
this is the greatest encouragement in the world to
rich people to lend a little money. It creates friends,
and it keeps them.

His shoes and boots were made in the best manner; this *got* him business; he set out with a rule to
tell no lies, and deceive no customers; this *secured*
his business. He had two reasons for not promising
to send home goods when he knew he should not be
able to keep his word. The first, because he knew
a lie was a sin, the next, because it was a folly.
There is no credit sooner worn out than that which
is gained by false pretences. After a little while no
one is deceived by them. Falsehood is so soon detected, that I believe most tradesmen are the poorer
for it in the long run. Deceit is the worst part of a
shopkeeper's stock in trade.

James was now at the head of a family. "This is

a serious situation," said he to himself, one fine summer's evening, as he stood leaning over the half door
of his shop to enjoy a little fresh air, " I am now
master of a family. My cares are doubled, and so
are my duties. I see the higher one gets in life the
more one has to answer for. Let me now call to
mind the sorrow I used to feel when I was made to
carry work home on a Sunday by an ungodly master,
and let me now keep the resolution I then formed."

So what his heart found right to do he resolved to
do quickly, and he set out at first as he meant to go
on. The Sunday was truly a day of rest at Mr.
Stock's. He would not allow a pair of shoes to be
given out on that day to oblige the best customer he
had. And what did he lose by it ? Why, nothing
For when the people were once used to it they liked
Saturday night just as well. But had it been otherwise he would have given up his gains to his conscience.

How Mr. Stock behaved to his Apprentices.

When he got up in the world so far as to have apprentices, he thought himself as accountable for their
behavior as if they had been his children. He was
very kind to them, and had a cheerful, merry way of
talking to them, so that the lads, who had seen too
much of swearing, reprobate masters, were fond of
him. They were never afraid of speaking to him ;
they told him all their little troubles, and considered
their master as their best friend, for they said they would
do anything for a good word and a kind look. As he
did not swear at them when they had been guilty of
a fault, they did not lie to him to conceal it, and
thereby make one fault two. But though he was
very kind he was very watchful also, for he did not
think neglect any part of kindness. He brought
them to adopt one very pretty method, which was,
on a Sunday evening to divert themselves with writing out half a dozen texts of Scripture.

When the boys carried him their books, he justly commended him whose texts were written in the fairest hand. "And now, my boys," said he, "let us see which of you will learn your texts best in the course of the week; he who does this shall choose for next Sunday." Thus the boys soon got many psalms and chapters by heart, almost without knowing how they came by them. He taught them how to make a practical use of what they learned, "for," said he, "it will answer little purposes to learn texts if we do not try to live up to them." One of the boys being apt to play in his absence, and to run back again to his work when he heard his master's step, he brought him to a sense of his fault by the last Sunday's text, which happened to be the sixth of Ephesians. He showed him what was meant by *being obedient to his master in singleness of heart as unto Christ,* and explained to him with so much kindness what it was *not to work with eye-service as men-pleasers, but doing the will of God from the heart,* that the lad said he should never forget it, and it did more toward curing him of idleness than the soundest horsewhipping would have done.

How Mr. Stock got out of Debt.

Stock's behavior was very regular, and he was much beloved for his kind and peaceable temper. He had also a good reputation for skill in his trade, and his industry was talked of through the whole town, so that he had soon more work than he could possibly do. He paid all his dealers to the very day, and took care to carry his interest money to the creditors the moment it became due. In two or three years he was able to begin to pay off a small part of the principal. His reason for being so eager to pay money as soon as it became due, was this: He had observed tradesmen, and especially his old master, put off the day of payment as long as they could, even though they had the means of paying in

8

their power. This deceived them—for having money in their pockets they forgot it belonged to the creditor and not to themselves, and so got to fancy they were rich when they were really poor. This false notion led them to indulge in idle expenses, whereas, if they had paid regularly, they would have had this one temptation the less. A young tradesman, when he is going to spend money, should at least ask himself, " Whether this money is his own or his creditors' ?" This little question might help to prevent many a bankruptcy.

A true Christian always goes heartily to work to find out what is his besetting sin ; and when he has found it (which he easily may if he looks sharp), against this sin he watches narrowly. Now I know it is the fashion among some folks (and a bad fashion it is), to fancy that good people have no sin ; but this only shows their ignorance. It is not true. That good man, Paul, knew better (Romans vii.). And when men do not own their sins, it is not because there is no sin in their hearts, but because they are not anxious to search for it, nor humble to confess it, nor penitent to mourn over it. But this was not the case with James Stock. " Examine yourselves truly," said he, " is no bad part of the catechism." He began to be afraid that his desire of living creditably, and without being a burden to any one, might, under the mask of honesty and independence, lead him into pride and covetousness. He feared that the bias of his heart lay that way. So instead of being proud of his sobriety; instead of bragging that he never spent his money idly, nor went to the alehouse ; instead of boasting how hard he worked and how he denied himself, he strove in secret that even these good qualities might not grow out of a wrong root. The following event was of use to him in the way of indulging any disposition to covetousness.

One evening as he was standing at the door of his shop, a poor dirty boy, without stockings and shoes,

came up and asked him for a bit of broken victuals,
for he had eaten nothing all day. In spite of his dirt
and rags, he was a very pretty, lively, civil-spoken
boy, and Mr. Stock could not help thinking he knew
something of his face. He fetched him out a good
piece of bread and cheese, and while he was devouring it, asked him if he had no parents, and why he
went about in that vagabond manner. "Daddy has
been dead some years," said the boy; "he died in a
fit over at the Grayhound. Mammy says he used to
live at this shop, and then we did not want for clothes
nor victuals neither." Stock was melted almost to
tears on finding that this dirty beggar-boy was Tommy
Williams, the son of his old master. He blessed God
on comparing his own happy condition with that of
this poor destitute child, but he was not prouder at
the comparison, and while he was thankful for his
own prosperity, he pitied the helpless boy. "Where
have you been living of late?" said he to him; "for
I understand you all went home to your mother's
friends."—"So we did, sir," said the boy; "but they
are grown tired of maintaining us, because they said
that mammy spent all the money which should have
gone to buy victuals for us, on snuff and drams; and
so they have sent us back to this place, which is
daddy's parish."

"And where do you live here?" said Mr. Stock.
"O sir, we are all put into the parish poorhouse."—
"And does your mother do anything to help to maintain you?"—"No, sir, for mammy says she was not
brought up to work like poor folks, and she would
rather starve than spin or knit; so she lies a-bed all
the morning, and sends us about to pick up what we
can, a bit of victuals or a few halfpence."—"And have
you any money in your pocket now?"—"Yes, sir, I
have got three halfpence which I have begged to-day."
"Then, as you were so very hungry, how came you
not to buy a roll at that baker's over the way?"—
"Because, sir, I was going to lay it out in tea for

mammy, for I never lay out a farthing for myself. In
deed, mammy says she *will* have her tea twice a day,
if we beg or starve for it."—"Can you read, my boy,"
said Mr. Stock. "A little, sir, and say my prayers
too."—"And can you say your catechism?"—"I
have almost forgotten it all, sir, though I remember
something about *honoring my father and mother*, and
that makes me still carry the halfpence home to mammy instead of buying cakes."—"Who taught you
these good things?"—"One Jemmy Stock, sir, who
was a parish 'prentice to my daddy. He taught me
one question out of the catechism every night, and
always made me say my prayers to him before I went
to bed. He told me I should go to the wicked place
if I did not fear God, so I am still afraid to tell lies
like the other boys. Poor Jemmy gave me a piece
of gingerbread every time I learnt well; but I have
no friend now; Jemmy was very good to me, though
mammy did nothing but beat him."

Mr. Stock was too much moved to carry on the
discourse. He did not make himself known to the
boy, but took him over to the baker's shop. As they
walked along, he could not help repeating aloud that
beautiful hymn, so deservedly the favorite of all children :

> "Not more than others I deserve,
>   Yet God has given me more ;
> For I have food while others starve,
>   Or beg from door to door."

The little boy looked up in his face, saying, "Why,
sir, that's the very hymn which Jemmy Stock gave
me a penny for learning." Stock made no answer,
but put a couple of threepenny loaves into his hand
to carry home, and told him to call on him again.

How Mr. Stock contrived to be charitable without any
expense.

Stock had abundant subject for meditation that
night. He was puzzled what to do with the boy

While he was carrying on his trade upon borrowed money, he did not think it right to give any part of that money to assist the idle, or even to help the distressed. "I must be just," said he, "before I am generous." Still he could not bear to see this fine boy given up to a certain ruin. He did not think it safe to take him into his shop in his present ignorant, unprincipled state. At last he hit upon this thought: "I work for myself twelve hours in the day. Why shall I not work one hour or two for this boy in the evening? It will be but for a year, and I shall then have more right to do what I please. My money will then be my own; I shall have paid my debts."

So he began to put his resolution in practice that very night, sticking to his old notion of not putting off till to-morrow what should be done to-day; and it was thought he owed much of his success in life, as well as his growth in goodness, to this little saying: "I am young and healthy," said he; "one hour's work more will do me no harm; I will set aside all I get by these overhours, and put the boy to school. I have not only no right to punish this child for the sins of his father, but I consider that though God hated those sins, he has made them to be instrumental to my advancement."

Tommy Williams called at the time appointed. In the meantime, Mr. Stock's maid had made him a neat little suit of clothes out of an old coat of her master's. She had also knit him a pair of stockings, and Mr. Stock made him sit down in the shop, while he fitted him with a pair of new shoes. The maid having washed and dressed him, Mr. Stock took him by the hand, and walked along with him to the parish poorhouse to find his mother. They found her dressed in ragged, filthy finery, standing at the door, where she passed most of her time, quarrelling with half a dozen women as idle and dirty as herself. When she saw Tommy so neat and well dressed, she fell a-crying for joy. She said "It put her in mind of old times;

for Tommy always used to be dressed like a gentleman."—"So much the worse," said Mr. Stock; "if
you had not begun by making him look like a gentleman, you needed not have ended by making him look
like a beggar."—"Oh Jem!" said she, for though it
was four years since she had seen him, she soon recollected him; "fine times for you! set a beggar on
horseback—you know the proverb. I shall beat
Tommy well for finding you out, and exposing me to
you."

Instead of entering into any dispute with this bad
woman, or praising himself at her expense; instead
of putting her in mind of her past ill behavior to him,
or reproaching her with the bad use she had made of
her prosperity, he mildly said to her, "Mrs. Williams,
I am sorry for your misfortunes; I am come to relieve you of part of your burden. I will take Tommy
off your hands. I will give him a year's board and
schooling, and by that time I shall see what he is fit
for. I will promise nothing, but if the boy turns out
well, I will never forsake him. I shall make but one
bargain with you, which is, that he must not come
to this place to hear all this railing and swearing, nor
shall he keep company with these pilfering idle children. You are welcome to go and see him when
you please, but here he must not come."

The foolish woman burst out a-crying, saying,
"she should lose her poor dear Tommy for ever.
Mr. Stock might give *her* the money he intended to
pay at the school, for nobody could do so well by him
as his own mother." The truth was, she wanted to
get these new clothes into her clutches, which would
all have been pawned at the dram-shop before the
week was out. This Mr. Stock well knew. From
crying she fell to scolding and swearing. She told
him he was an unnatural wretch, that wanted to make
a child despise his own mother because she was poor.
She even went so far as to say she would not part
from him; she said she hated your godly people, they

had no bowels of compassion, but tried to set men, women, and children, against their own flesh and blood.

Mr. Stock now almost lost his patience, and for one moment a thought came across him, to strip the boy, carry back the clothes, and leave him to his unnatural mother. "Why," said he, "should I work over-hours, and wear out my strength for this wicked woman?" But soon he checked his thought, by reflecting on the patience and long-suffering of God with rebellious sinners. This cured his anger in a moment, and he mildly reasoned with her on the folly and blindness in opposing the good of her child.

One of the neighbors who stood by said, "What a fine thing it was for the boy! but some people were born to be lucky. She wished Mr. Stock would take a fancy to *her* child, he should have him soon enough." Mrs. Williams now began to be frightened lest Mr. Stock should take the woman at her word, and sullenly consented to let the boy go, from envy and malice, not from prudence and gratitude; and Tommy was sent to school that very night, his mother crying and roaring, instead of thanking God for such a blessing.

Here I can not forbear telling a very good-natured thing of Will Simpson, one of the workmen. By-the-by, it was that very young fellow who was reformed by Stock's good example, when he was an apprentice, and who used to sing psalms with him on a Sunday evening, when they got out of the way of Williams's junketing. Will coming home early one evening, was surprised to find his master at work by himself, long after the usual time. He begged so heartily to know the reason, that Stock owned the truth. Will was so struck with this piece of kindness, that he snatched up a last, crying out, "Well, master, you shall not work by yourself, however; we will go snacks in maintaining Tommy: it shall never be said that Will Simpson was idling about when his master was working for charity." This made the hour pass cheerfully, and doubled the profits.

In a year or two, Mr. Stock, by God's blessing on his labors, became quite clear of the world. He now paid off his creditors, but he never forgot his obligation to them, and found many opportunities of showing kindness to them, and to their children after them. He now cast about for a proper wife, and as he was thought a prosperous man, and was very well looking besides, most of the smart girls of the place, with their tawdry finery, used to be often parading before the shop, and would even go to chuch in order to put themselves in his way. But Mr. Stock, when he went to church, had other things in his head; and if ever he thought about these gay damsels at all, it was with concern in seeing them so improperly tricked out, so that the very means they took to please him. made him dislike them.

There was one Betsy West, a young woman of excellent character, and very modest appearance. He had seldom seen her out, as she was employed night and day in waiting on an aged widowed mother, who was both lame and blind. This good girl was indeed almost literally eyes and feet to her helpless parent, and Mr. Stock used to ee her, through the little casement window, lifting her up, and feeding with a tenderness which greatly raised his esteem for her. He used to tell Will Simpson, as they sat at work, that such a dutiful daughter could hardly help to make a faithful wife. He had not, however, the heart to try to draw her off from her care of her sick mother. The poor woman declined very fast. Betsy was much employed in reading or praying by her, while she was awake, and passed a good part of the night while she slept, in doing some fine works to sell, in order to supply her sick mother with little delicacies which their poor pittance could not afford, while she herself lived on a crust.

Mr. Stock knew that Betsy would have little or

nothing after her mother's death. as she had only a
life income.   On the other hand, Mr. Thompson, the
tanner, had offered him two hundred pounds with his
daughter Nancy; but he was almost sorry that he
had not in this case an opportunity of resisting his
natural bias, which rather lay on the side of loving
money : " For," said he, " putting principle and putting affection out of the question, I shall do a more
prudent thing by marrying Betsy West, who will
conform to her station, and is a religious, humble, industrious girl, without a shilling, than by having an
idle dressy lass, who will neglect my family and fill
my house with company, though she should have
twice the fortune which Nancy Thompson would
bring."

At length poor old Mrs. West was released from
all her sufferings.   At a proper time Mr. Stock proposed marriage to Betsy, and was accepted.   All the
disappointed girls in the town wondered what anybody could like in such a dowdy as that.   Had the
man no eyes ?   They thought Mr. Stock had had
more taste.   Oh! how did it provoke all the vain idle
things to find that staying at home, dressing plainly,
serving God, and nursing a blind mother, should do
that for Betsy West, which all their contrivances,
flaunting, and dancing, could not do for them.

He was not disappointed in his hope of meeting
with a good wife in Betsy, as indeed those who marry
on right grounds seldom are.   But if religious per-
sons will, for the sake of money, choose partners for
life who have no religion, do not let them complain
that they are unhappy ; they might have known that
beforehand.

Tommy Williams was now taken home to Stock's
house and bound apprentice.   He was always kind
and attentive to his mother; and every penny which
Will Simpson or his master gave him for learning a
chapter, he would save to buy a bit of tea and sugar
for her.   When the other boys laughed at him fo

being so foolish as to deny himself cakes and apples to give his money to her who was so bad a woman, he would answer, " It may be so, but she is my mother for all that."

Mr. Stock was much moved at the change in this boy, who turned out a very good youth. He resolved, as God should prosper him, that he would try to snatch other helpless creatures from sin and ruin. " For," said he, " it is owing to God's blessing on the instructions of my good minister when I was a child, that I have been saved from the broad way of destruction." He still gave God the glory of everything he did aright : and when Will Simpson one day said to him, " Master, I wish I were half as good as you are ;" " Hold, William," answered he gravely, " I once read in a book, that the devil is willing enough we should appear to do good actions, if he can but make us proud of them."

The frolics of idle Jack Brown.

You shall now hear what befell idle Jack Brown, who, being a farmer's son, had many advantages to begin life with. But he who wants prudence may be said to want everything, because he turns all his advantages to no account.

Jack Brown was just out of his time when his master Williams died in that terrible drunken fit at the Grayhound. You know already how Stock succeeded to his master's business, and prospered in it. Jack wished very much to enter into partnership with him. His father and mother too were desirous of it, and offered to advance a hundred pounds with him. Here is a fresh proof of the power of character! The old farmer, with all his covetousness, was eager to get his son into partnership with Stock, though the latter was not worth a shilling ; and even Jack's mother, with all her pride, was eager for it, for they had both sense enough to see it would be the making of Jack. The father knew that Stock would look to the main chance ; and the mother that he would take the laboring oar, and so her darling would have little to do. The ruling passion operated in both. One parent wished to secure to the son a life of pleasure, the other a profitable trade. Both were equally indifferent to whatever related to his eternal good.

Stock, however, young as he was, was too old a bird to be caught with chaff. His wisdom was an overmatch for their cunning. He had a kindness for Brown, but would on no account enter into business with him.—"One of these three things," said he, "I am sure will happen if I do; he will either hurt my principles, my character, or my trade; perhaps all." And here let me drop a hint to young men who are about to enter into partnership. Let them not do that in haste which they may repent at leisure. Next to marriage it is a tie the hardest to break ; and next to that it is an engagement which ought to be entered into with the most caution. Many things go to the making such a connexion suitable, safe, and pleasant. There is many a rich merchant need not be above taking a hint in this respect, from James Stock, the shoemaker.

Brown was still unwilling to part from him ; indeed he was too idle to look out for business, so he offered Stock to work with him as a journeyman, but this he also mildly refused. It hurt his good-nature to do so ; but he reflected that a young man who has his way to make in the world must not only be good-natured, he must be prudent also. " I am resolved," said he, "to employ none but the most sober, regular young men I can get. Evil communications corrupt good manners, and I should be answerable for all the disorders of my house, if I knowingly took a wild drinking young fellow into it. That which might be kindness to one would be injustice to many, and therefore a sin in myself."

Brown's mother was in a great rage when she

heard that her son had stooped so low as to make this offer. She valued herself on being proud, for she thought pride was a grand thing. Poor woman. She did not know that it is the meanest thing in the world. It was her ignorance which made her proud, as is apt to be the case.—"You mean-spirited rascal," said she to Jack, "I had rather follow you to your grave, as well as I love you, than see you disgrace your family by working under Jem Stock, the parish-apprentice." She forgot already what pains she had taken about the partnership, but pride and passion have bad memories.

It is hard to say which was now uppermost in her mind, her desire to be revenged on Stock, or to see her son make a figure. She raised every shilling she could get from her husband, and all she could crib from the dairy to set up Jack in a showy way. So the very next market day she came herself, and took for him the new white house, with the two sash windows painted blue, and blue posts before the door. It is that house which has the old cross just before it, as you turn down between the church and the Gray-hound. Its being so near the church to be sure was no recommendation to Jack, but its being so near the Grayhound was, and so taking one thing with the other, it was to be sure no bad situation; but what weighed most with the mother was, that it was a much more showy shop than Stock's; and the house, though not half so convenient, was far more smart.

In order to draw custom, his foolish mother advised him to undersell his neighbors just at first; to buy ordinary but showy goods, and to employ cheap workmen. In short she charged him to leave no stone unturned to ruin his old comrade Stock. Indeed she always thought with double satisfaction of Jack's prosperity, because she always joined to it the hope that his success would be the ruin of Stock, for she owned it would be the joy of her heart to bring that proud upstart to a morsel of bread. She did not understand, for her part, why such beggars must become tradesmen.

Stock, however, set out on quite another set of principles. He did not allow himself to square his own behavior to others by theirs to him. He seldom asked himself what he should *like* to do : but he had a mighty way of saying, I wonder now what is my *duty* to do ?—And when he was once clear in that matter he generally did it, always begging God's blessing and direction. So instead of setting Brown at defiance; instead of all that vulgar selfishness of catch-he that catch-can—and two of a trade can never agree—he resolved to be friendly toward him. Instead of joining in the laugh against Brown for making his house so fine, he was sorry for him, because he feared he would never be able to pay such a rent. He very kindly called upon him, told him there was business enough for them both, and gave him many useful hints for his going on. He warned him to go oftener to church and seldomer to the Grayhound : put him in mind how following the one and forsaking the other had been the ruin of their poor master, and added the following advice to young tradesmen :—

Buy the best goods ; cut the work out yourself ; let the eye of the master be everywhere ; employ the soberest men ; avoid all the low deceits of trade ; never lower the credit of another to raise your own ; make short payments ; keep exact accounts ; avoid idle company, and be very strict to your word.

For a short time things went on swimmingly. Brown was merry and civil. The shop was well situated for gossip ; and every one who had something to say, and nothing to do, was welcome. Every idle story was first spread, and every idle song first sung in Brown's shop. Every customer who came to be measured was promised that his shoes should be done first. But the misfortune was, if twenty came in a day the same promise was made to all ; so

9

that nineteen were disappointed, and of course af
fronted. He never said *no* to any one. It is indeed
a word which it requires some honesty to pronounce.
By all these false promises he was thought the most
obliging fellow that ever made a shoe. And as he set
out on the principle of underselling, people took a
mighty fancy to the cheap shop. And it was agreed
among all the young and giddy, that he would beat
Stock hollow, and that the old shop would soon be
knocked up.

All is not gold that glistens.

After a few months, however, folks began to be not
quite so fond of the cheap shop ; one found out that
the leather was bad, another that the work was slight.
Those who liked substantial goods went all of them
to Stock's, for they said Brown's heel taps did not
last a week ; his new boots let in water, and they
believed he made his soles of brown paper. Besides,
it was thought by most that this promising all, and
keeping his word with none, hurt his business as
much as anything. Indeed, I question, putting religion out of the question, if lying ever answers, even
in a political view.

Brown had what is commonly called a *good heart*,
that is, he had a thoughtless good nature, and a sort
of feeling for the moment which made him very sorry when others were in trouble. But he was not
apt to put himself to any inconvenience, nor go a step
out of his way, nor give up any pleasure to serve the
best friend he had. He loved *fun ;* and those who do
should always see that it be harmless, and that they
do not give up more for it than it is worth. I am
not going to say a word against innocent merriment.
I like it myself. But what the proverb says of gold,
may be said of mirth—it may be bought too dear. If
a young man finds that what he fancies is a good joke
may possibly offend God, hurt his neighbor, afflict
his parent, or make a modest girl blush, let him then

be assured it is not fun, but wickedness, and he had better let it alone.

Jack Brown, then, as *good a heart* as he had, did not know what it was to deny himself anything. He was so *good-natured*, indeed, that he never in his life refused to make one of a jolly set; but he was not good-natured enough to consider that those men whom he kept up all night roaring and laughing, had wives and children at home, who had little to eat, and less to wear, because *they* were keeping up the character of merry fellows, and good hearts, at the public house.

The Mountebank.

One day he saw his father's plough-boy come galloping up to the door in great haste. This boy brought Brown word that his mother was dangerously ill, and that his father had sent his own best bay mare, Smiler, that his son might lose no time, but set out directly to see his mother before she died. Jack burst into tears, lamented the danger of so fond a mother, and all the people in the shop extolled his *good heart.*

He sent back the boy directly, with a message that he would follow him in half an hour, as soon as the mare had baited, for he well knew that his father would not thank him for any haste he might make if Smiler was hurt.

Jack accordingly set off, and rode with such speed to the next town, that both himself and Smiler had a mind to another bait. They stopped at the Star; unluckily it was fair-day, and as he was walking about while Smiler was eating her oats, a bill was put into his hand, setting forth, that on the stage opposite the globe a mountebank was showing away, and his andrew performing the finest tricks that ever were seen. He read—he stood still—he went on—"It will not hinder me," says he, " Smiler must rest, and I shall see my poor dear mother quite as soon if I just take a peep, as if I sit moping at the Star."

The tricks were so merry that the t me seemed short, and when they were over he could not forbear going into the Globe and treating these choice spirits with a bowl of punch.   Just as they were taking the last glass Jack happened to say that he was the best fives player in the country.   "That is lucky," said the andrew, "for there is a famous match now playing in the court, and you may never again have such an opportunity to show your skill."   Brown declared "he could not stay, for that he had left his horse at the Star, and must set off on urgent business."   They now all pretended to call his skill in question.   This roused his pride, and he thought another half hour could break no squares.   Smiler had now had a good feed of corn, and he would only have to push her on a little more, so to it he went.

He won the first game.   This spurred him on, and he played till it was so dark they could not see a ball.   Another bowl was called for from the winner. Wagers and bets now drained Brown not only of all the money he had won, but of all he had in his pocket, so that he was obliged to ask leave to go to the house where his horse was, to borrow enough to discharge his reckoning at the Globe.

All these losses brought his poor dear mother to his mind, and he marched off with rather a heavy heart to borrow the money, and to order Smiler out of the stable.   The landlord expressed much surprise at seeing him, and the ostler declared there was no Smiler there—that he had been rode off above two hours ago by the merry-andrew, who said he came by order of the owner, Mr. Brown, to fetch him to the Globe, and to pay for his feed.   It was indeed one of the neatest tricks the andrew ever performed, for he made such a clean conveyance of Smiler, that neither Jack nor his father ever heard of her again.

It was night; no one could tell what road the andrew took, and it was another hour or two before an advertisement could be drawn up for apprehending the horse-stealer. Jack had some doubts whether he should go on or return back. He knew that though his father might fear his wife most, yet he loved Smiler best. At length he took that courage from a glass of brandy which he ought to have taken from a hearty repentance, and he resolved to pursue his journey. He was obliged to leave his watch and silver buckles in pawn for a little old hack which was nothing but skin and bone, and would hardly trot three miles an hour.

He knocked at his father's door about five in the morning. The family were all up. He asked the boy who opened the door, how his mother was. "She is dead," said the boy; "she died yesterday afternoon." Here Jack's heart smote him, and he cried aloud, partly from grief, but more from the reproaches of his own conscience, for he found by computing the hours, that had he come straight on he should have been in time to receive his mother's blessing.

The farmer now came from within; "I hear Smiler's step. Is Jack come?" "Yes, father," said Jack, in a low voice. "Then," cried the farmer, "run every man and boy of you and take care of the mare. Tom, do thou go and rub her down; Jem, run and get her a good feed of corn. Be sure walk her about that she may not catch cold." Young Brown came in. "Are you not an undutiful dog?" said the father; "you might have been here twelve hours ago. Your mother could not die in peace without seeing you. She said it was cruel return for all her fondness that you could not make a little haste to see her; but it was always so, for she had wronged her other children to help you, and this was her reward." Brown sobbed out a few words, but his father replied, "Never cry, Jack, for the boy told me that it was out of regard for Smiler that you were not here as soon as he was, and if 'twas your over

care of her, why, there's no great harm done. You
could not have saved your poor mother, and you
might have hurt the mare." Here Jack's double
guilt flew into his face. He knew that his father
was very covetous, and had lived on bad terms with
his wife, and also that his own unkindness to her
had been forgiven by him out of love to the horse,
but to break to him how he had lost that horse
through his own folly and want of feeling, was more
than Jack had courage to do. The old man, however, soon got at the truth, and no words can describe his fury. Forgetting that his wife lay dead
above stairs, he abused his son in a way not fit to be
repeated, and though his covetousness had just before found an excuse for a favorite son neglecting to
visit a dying parent, yet he now vented his rage
against Jack as an unnatural brute, whom he would
cut off without a shilling, and bade him never see his
face again.

Jack was not allowed to attend his mother's funeral,
which was a real grief to him; nor would his father
advance even the little money which was needful to
redeem his things at the Star. He had now no fond
mother to assist him, and he set out on his return
home on his borrowed hack, full of grief. He had
the added mortification of knowing, that he had also
lost by his folly a little hoard of money which his
mother had saved up for him.

When Brown got back to his own town he found
that the story of Smiler and the andrew had got
thither before him, and it was thought a very good
joke at the Grayhound. He soon recovered his
spirits as far as related to the horse, but as to his behavior to his dying mother it troubled him at times
to the last day of his life, though he did all he could
to forget it. He did not, however, go on at all better, nor did he engage in one frolic the less for what
had passed at the Globe; his *good heart* continually
betrayed him into acts of levity and vanity.

Jack began at length to feel the reverse of that proverb, *Keep your shop and your shop will keep you.* He had neglected his customers, and they forsook him. Quarter-day came round; there was much to pay and little to receive. He owed two years' rent. He was in arrears to his men for wages. He had a long account with his currier. It was in vain to apply to his father. He had now no mother. Stock was the only true friend he had in the world, and had helped him out of many petty scrapes—but he knew Stock would advance no money in so hopeless a case. Duns came fast about him. He named a speedy day for payment, but as soon as they were out of the house, and the danger put off to a little distance, he forgot every promise, was as merry as ever, and run the same round of thoughtless gayety. Whenever he was in trouble Stock did not shun him, because that was the moment to throw in a little good advice. He one day asked him if he always intended to go on in this course. "No," said he, " I am resolved by-and-by to reform, grow sober, and go to church. Why, I am but five-and-twenty, man, I am stout and healthy, and likely to live long; I can repent, and grow melancholy and good at any time."

"Oh, Jack," said Stock, "don't cheat thyself with that false hope. What thou dost intend to do, do quickly. Didst thou never read about the heart growing hardened by long indulgence in sin! Some folk, who pretend to mean well, show that they mean nothing at all, by never beginning to put their good resolutions into practice, which made a wise man once say, that hell is paved with good intentions. We can not repent when we please. *It is the goodness of God which leadeth us to repentance.*"

" I am sure," replied Jack, " I am no one's enemy but my own."

" It is as foolish," said Stock, " to say a bad man is no one's enemy but his own, as that a good man is no one's friend but his own. There is no such neutral character. A bad man corrupts or offends all within reach of his example, just as a good man benefits or instructs all within the sphere of his influence. And there is no time when we can say that this transmitted good and evil will end. A wicked man may be punished for sins he never committed himself, if he has been the cause of sin in others, as surely as a saint will be rewarded for more good deeds that he himself has done, even for the virtues and good actions of all those who are made better by his instructions, his example, or his writings."

Michaelmas-day was at hand. The landlord declared he would be put off no longer, but would seize for rent if it was not paid him on that day, as well as for a considerable sum due to him for leather. Brown at last began to be frightened. He applied to Stock to be bound for him. This, Stock flatly refused. Brown now began to dread the horrors of a jail, and really seemed so very contrite, and made so many vows and promises of amendment, that at length Stock was prevailed on, together with two or three of Brown's other friends, to advance each a small sum of money to quiet the landlord, Brown promising to make over to them every part of his stock, and to be guided in future by their advice, declaring that he would turn over a new leaf, and follow Mr. Stock's example, as well as his direction in everything.

Stock's good nature was at length wrought upon, and he raised the money. The truth is, he did not know the worst, nor how deeply Brown was involved. Brown joyfully set out on the very quarter-day to a town at some distance, to carry his landlord this money, raised by the imprudent kindness of his friend. At his departure Stock put him in mind of the old story of Smiler and the merry-andrew, and he promised of his own head that he would not even call at a public house till he had paid the money.

He was as good as his word. He very triumphant-
ly passed by several. He stopped a little under the
window of one where the sounds of merriment and
loud laughter caught his ear. At another he heard
the enticing notes of a fiddle, and the light heels of
the merry dancers. Here his heart had well nigh
failed him; but the dread of a jail on the one hand,
and what he feared almost as much, Mr. Stock's
anger on the other, spurred him on, and he valued
himself not a little at having got the better of this
temptation. He felt quite happy when he found he
had reached the door of his landlord without having
yielded to one idle inclination.

He knocked at the door. The maid who opened
it said her master was not at home. "I am sorry for
it," said he, strutting about; and with a boasting air
he took out his money. "I want to pay him my
rent: he needed not to have been afraid of *me*." The
servant, who knew her master was very much afraid
of him, desired him to walk in, for her master would
be at home in half an hour. "I will call again," said
he; "but no, let him call on me, and the sooner the
better: I shall be at the Blue Posts." While he had
been talking, he took care to open his black leather
case, and to display the bank bills to the servant, and
then in a swaggering way, he put up his money and
marched off to the Blue Posts.

He was by this time quite proud of his own resolution, and having tendered the money, and being clear
in his own mind that it was the landlord's own fault
and not his that it was not paid, he went to refresh
himself at the Blue Posts. In a barn belonging to
this public house, a set of strollers were just going to
perform some of that sing-song ribaldry by which our
villages are corrupted, the laws broken, and that money
drawn from the poor for pleasure, which is wanted by
their families for bread. The name of the last new
song, which made part of the entertainment, made
him think himself in high luck, that he should have

just that half hour to spare. He went into the barn, but
was too much delighted with the actor, who sung his
favorite song, to remain a quiet hearer. He leaped out
of the pit, and got behind the two ragged blankets
which served for a curtain. He sung so much better
than the actors themselves, that they praised and ad-
mired him to a degree which awakened all his vanity.
He was so intoxicated with their flattery, that he could
do no less than invite them all to supper, an invitation
which they were too hungry not to accept.

He did not, however, quite forget his appointment
with his landlord; but the half hour was long since
past by. "And so," says he, "as I know he is a
mean curmudgeon, who goes to bed by daylight to
save candles, it will be too late to speak with him to-
night; besides, let him call upon me; it is his business and not mine. I left word where I was to be
found; the money is ready, and if I don't pay him
to-night, I can do it before breakfast."

By the time these firm resolutions were made, supper was ready. There never was a more jolly evening. Ale and punch were as plentiful as water. The
actors saw what a vain fellow was feasting them: and
as they wanted victuals and he wanted flattery, the
business was soon settled. They ate, and Brown
sung. They pretended to be in raptures. Singing
promoted drinking, and every fresh glass produced
a song or a story still more merry than the former.
Before morning, the players, who were engaged to
act in another barn a dozen miles off, stole away
quietly. Brown having dropt asleep, they left him to
finish his nap by himself. As to him, his dreams
were gay and pleasant, and the house being quite still,
he slept comfortably till morning.

As soon as he had breakfasted, the business of the
night before popped into his head. He set off once
more to his landlord's in high spirits, gayly singing
by the way scraps of all the tunes he had picked up
the night before from his new friends. The landlord

opened the door himself, and reproached him with no small surliness for not having kept his word with him the evening before, adding, that he supposed he was come now with some more of his shallow excuses. Brown put on all that haughtiness which is common to people who being generally apt to be in the wrong, happen to catch themselves doing a right action ; he looked big, as some sort of people do when they have money to pay. " You need not have been so anxious about your money," said he, " I was not going to break or run away." The landlord well knew this was the common language of those who are ready to do both. Brown haughtily added, " You shall see I am a man of my word : give me a receipt." The landlord had it ready and gave it him.

Brown put his hand in his pocket for his black leathern case in which the bills were: he felt, he searched, he examined, first one pocket, then the other, then both waistcoat pockets, but no leather case could he find. He looked terrified. It was indeed the face of real terror, but the landlord conceived it to be that of guilt, and abused him heartily for putting his old tricks upon him ; he swore he would not be imposed upon any longer ; the money or a jail— there lay his choice.

Brown protested for once with great truth, that he had no intention to deceive ; declared that he had actually brought the money, and knew not what was become of it ; but the thing was far too unlikely to gain credit. Brown now called to mind that he had fallen asleep on the settle in the room where they had supped. This raised his spirits, for he had no doubt but the case had fallen out of his pocket. He said he would step to the public house and search for it, and would be back directly. Not one word of this did the landlord believe, so inconvenient is it to have a bad character. He swore Brown should not stir out of his house without a constable, and made him wai while he sent for one. Brown, guarded by the consta

ble, went back to the Blue Posts, the landlord charging the officer not to lose sight of the culprit. The
caution was needless: Brown had not the least de-
sign of running away, so firmly persuaded was he
that he should find his leather case.

But who can paint his dismay, when no tale or tidings of the leather case could be had? The master,
the mistress, the boy, the maid of the public house,
all protested they were innocent. His suspicions
soon fell on the strollers with whom he had passed the
night; and he now found out for the first time, that a
merry evening did not always produce a happy morning. He obtained a warrant, and proper officers were
sent in pursuit of the strollers. No one, however,
believed he had really lost anything; and as he had
not a shilling left to defray the expensive treat he had
given, the master of the inn agreed with the other
landlord in thinking this story was a trick to defraud
them both, and Brown remained in close custody.
At length the officers returned, who said they had
been obliged to let the strollers go, as they could not
fix the charge on any one, and they had offered to
swear before a justice that they had seen nothing of the
leather case. It was at length agreed, that as he had
passed the evening in a crowded barn, he had probably been robbed there, if at all; and among so many,
who could pretend to guess at the thief?

Brown raved like a madman; he cried, tore his
hair, and said he was ruined for ever. The abusive
language of his old landlord, and his new creditor at
the Blue Posts, did not lighten his sorrow. His landlord would be put off no longer. Brown declared he
could neither find bail nor raise another shilling; and
as soon as the forms of law were made out, he was
sent to the county jail.

Here it might have been expected that hard living
and much leisure would have brought him to reflect a
little on his past follies. But his heart was not truly
touched. The chief thing which grieved him at first

was, his having abused the kindness of Stock, for to him he should appear guilty of a real fraud, where he had indeed been only vain, idle, and imprudent. Vanity, idleness, and imprudence, often bring a man to utter ruin both of soul and body, though silly people do not put them in the catalogue of heavy sins; and those who indulge in them are often reckoned honest, merry fellows, with *the best hearts in the world.*

Jack Brown in Prison

Brown was no sooner lodged in his doleful habitation, and a little recovered from his first surprise, than he sat down and wrote his friend Stock the whole history of the transaction. Mr. Stock, who had long known the exceeding lightness and dissipation of his mind, did not so utterly disbelieve the story as all the other creditors did. To speak the truth, Stock was the only one among them who had good sense enough to know, that a man may be completely ruined, both in what relates to his property and his soul, without committing Old-Bailey crimes. He well knew that idleness, vanity, and the love of *pleasure*, as it is falsely called, will bring a man to a morsel of bread, as surely as those things which are reckoned much greater sins, and that they undermine his principles as certainly, though not quite so fast.

Stock was too angry with what had happened to answer Brown's letter, or to seem to take the least notice of him. However, he kindly and secretly undertook a journey to the hard-hearted old farmer, Brown's father, to intercede with him, and to see if he would do anything for his son. Stock did not pretend to excuse Jack, or even to lessen his offences; for it was a rule of his never to disguise truth or to palliate wickedness. Sin was still sin in his eyes, though it were committed by his best friend; but though he would not soften the sin, he felt tenderly for the sinner. He pleaded with the old farmer on the ground, that his son's idleness and other vices would gather fresh strength in a jail. He told him that the loose and worthless company which he would there keep, would harden him in vice, and if he was now wicked, he might there become irreclaimable.

But all his pleas were urged in vain. The farmer was not to be moved; indeed, he argued with some justice, that he ought not to make his industrious children beggars to save one rogue from the gallows. Mr. Stock allowed the force of his reasoning, though he saw the father was less influenced by this principle of justice than by resentment on account of the old story of Smiler. People, indeed, should take care that what appears in their conduct to proceed from justice, does not proceed really from revenge. Wiser men than Farmer Brown often deceive themselves, and fancy they act on better principles than they really do, for want of looking a little more closely into their own hearts, and putting down every action to its true motive. When we are praying against deceit, we should not forget to take self-deceit into the account.

Mr. Stock at length wrote to poor Jack : not to offer him any help, that was quite out of the question, but to exhort him to repent of his evil ways, to lay before him the sins of his past life, and to advise him to convert the present punishment into a benefit, by humbling himself before God. He offered his interest to get his place of confinement exchanged for one of those improved prisons, where solitude and labor have been made the happy instruments of bringing many to a better way of thinking, and ended by saying, that if he ever gave any solid signs of real amendment, he would still be his friend, in spite of all that was past.

If Mr. Stock had sent him a good sum of money to procure his liberty, or even to make merry with his wretched companions, Jack would have thought him a friend indeed. But to send him nothing but dry advice, and a few words of empty comfort, was, he thought, but a cheap shabby way of showing his kindness Unluckily, the letter came just as he was going to sit down to one of those direful merry-makings which are often carried on with brutal riot within the doleful walls of a jail on the entrance of a new prisoner. who is often expected to give a feast to the rest.

When his companions were heated with gin, " Now," said Jack, " I'll treat you with a sermon, and a very pretty preachment it is." So saying, he took out Mr. Stock's kind and pious letter, and was delighted at the bursts of laughter it produced. " What a canting dog!" said one. " Repentance, indeed!" cried Tom Crew ; " No, no, Jack, tell this hypocritical rogue that if we have lost our liberty, it is only for having been jolly, hearty fellows, and we have more spirit than to repent of that, I hope : all the harm we have done is living a little too fast, like honest bucks as we are."—" Ay, ay," said jolly George, " had we been such sneaking miserly fellows as Stock, we need not have come hither. But if the ill nature of the laws has been so cruel as to clap up such fine hearty blades, we are no *felons* however. We are afraid of no Jack Ketch; and I see no cause to repent of any sin that's not hanging matter. As to those who are thrust into the condemned hole indeed, and have but a few hours to live, they *must* see the parson, and hear a sermon, and such stuff. But I do not know what such stout young fellows as we are have to do with repentance. And so, Jack, let us have that rare new catch which you learnt of the strollers that merry night when you lost your pocket-book.

This thoughtless youth soon gave a fresh proof of the power of evil company, and of the quick progress of the heart of a sinner from bad to worse. Brown, who always wanted principle, soon grew to want feeling also. He joined in the laugh which was raised against Stock, and told many *good stories*, as they were called, in derision of the piety, sobriety, and self-denial of his old friend. He lost every day somewhat

of those small remains of shame and decency which
he had brought with him to the prison. He even
grew reconciled to this wretched way of life, and the
want of money seemed to him the heaviest evil in the
life of a jail.

Mr. Stock finding from the jailer that his letter had
been treated with ridicule, would not write to him
any more. He did not come to see him nor send
him any assistance, thinking it right to let him suffer
that want which his vices had brought upon him.
But as he still hoped that the time would come when
he might be brought to a sense of his evil courses, he
continued to have an eye upon him by means of the
jailer, who was an honest, kind-hearted man.

Brown spent one part of his time in thoughtless
riot, and the other in gloomy sadness. Company
kept up his spirits; with his new friends he contrived
to drown thought; but when he was alone he began
to find that a *merry fellow*, when deprived of his companions and his liquor, is often a most forlorn wretch.
Then it is that even a merry fellow says, "*Of laughter,
what is it? and of mirth, it is madness.*"

As he contrived, however, to be as little alone as
possible, his gayety was commonly uppermost till
that loathsome distemper, called the jail fever, broke
out in the prison. Tom Crew, the ringleader in all
their evil practices, was first seized with it. Jack
stayed a little while with his comrade to assist and
divert him, but of assistance he could give little, and
the very thought of diversion was now turned into
horror. He soon caught the distemper, and that in
so dreadful a degree, that his life was in great danger.
Of those who remained in health, not a soul came
near him, though he shared his last farthing with
them. He had just sense enough left to feel this
cruelty. Poor fellow! he did not know before, that
the friendship of the worldly is at an end when there is
no more drink or diversion to be had. He lay in the
most deplorable condition; his body tormented with

ᴀ dreadful disease, and his soul terrified and amazed at the approach of death: that death which he thought at so great a distance, and of which his comrades had so often assured him, that a young fellow of five-and-twenty was in no danger. Poor Jack! I can not help feeling for him. Without a shilling! without a friend! without one comfort respecting this world, and, what is far more terrible, without one hope respecting the next.

Let not the young reader fancy that Brown's misery arose entirely from his altered circumstances. It was not merely his being in want, and sick, and in prison, which made his condition so desperate. Many an honest man unjustly accused, many a persecuted saint, many a holy martyr, has enjoyed sometimes more peace and content in a prison, than wicked men have ever tasted in the height of their prosperity. But to any such comforts, to any comfort at all, poor Jack was an utter stranger.

A Christian friend generally comes forward at the very time when worldly friends forsake the wretched. The other prisoners would not come near Brown, though he had often entertained, and had never offended them; even his own father was not moved with his sad condition. When Mr. Stock informed him of it, he answered, "'Tis no more than he deserves. As he brews, so he must bake. He has made his own bed, and let him lie in it." The hard old man had ever at his tongue's end some proverb of hardness or frugality, which he contrived to turn in such a way as to excuse himself.

We shall now see how Mr. Stock behaved. He had his favorite sayings too; but they were chiefly on the side of kindness, mercy, or some other virtue. "I must not," said he, "pretend to call myself a Christian, if I do not requite evil with good." When he received the jailer's letter with the account of Brown's sad condition, Will Simpson and Tommy Williams began to compliment him on his own wis-

dom and prudence, by which he had escaped Brown's
misfortunes. He only gravely said, " Blessed be God
that I am not in the same misery. It is *he* who has
made us to differ. But for *his* grace I might have
been in no better condition. Now Brown is brought
low by the hand of God, it is my time to go to him."
" What, you!" said Will, "whom he cheated of
your money?"—"This is not a time to remember
injuries," said Mr. Stock. "How can I ask forgiveness for my own sins, if I withhold forgiveness from
him!" So saying, he ordered his horse, and set off
to see poor Brown, thus proving that his was a religion not of words but of deeds.

Stock's heart nearly failed him as he passed through
the prison. The groans of the sick and dying, and,
what to him was still more moving, the brutal merriment of the healthy in such a place, pierced his very
soul. Many a silent prayer did he put up as he
passed along, that God would yet be pleased to touch
their hearts, and that now (during this infectious sickness) might be the accepted time. The jailer observed him drop a tear, and asked the cause. " I can
not forget," said he, "that the most dissolute of these
men is still my fellow-creature. The same God made
them; the same Savior died for them; how then can
I hate the worst of them? With my advantages they
might have been much better than I am; without the
blessing of God on my good minister's instructions,
I might have been worse that the worst of these. I
have no cause for pride, much for thankfulness; *let
us not be high-minded, but fear.*"

It would have moved a heart of stone to have seen
poor miserable Jack Brown lying on his wretched
bed, his face so changed by pain, poverty, dirt, and
sorrow, that he could hardly be known for that merry
soul of a jack-boot, as he used to be proud to hear
himself called. His groans were so piteous that it
made Mr. Stock's heart ache. He kindly took him
by the hand, though he knew the distemper was

catching. "How dost do, Jack?" said he; "dost know me?" Brown shook his head and said, faintly. "Know you? ay, that I do. I am sure I have but one friend in the world who would come to see me in this woful condition. O James! what have I brought myself to? What will become of my poor soul? I dare not look back, for that is all sin, nor forward, for that is all misery and wo."

Mr. Stock spake kindly to him, but did not attempt to cheer him with false comfort, as is too often done. "I am ashamed to see you in this dirty place," says Brown. "As to the place, Jack," replied the other, "if it has helped to bring you to a sense of your past offences, it will be no bad place for you. I am heartily sorry for your distress and your sickness; but if it should please God by them to open your eyes, and to show you that sin is a greater evil than the prison to which it has brought you, all may yet be well. I had rather see you in this humble, penitent state, lying on this dirty bed, in this dismal prison, than roaring and rioting at the Grayhound, the king of the company, with handsome clothes on your back, and plenty of money in your pocket."

Brown wept bitterly, and squeezed his hand, but was too weak to say much. Mr. Stock then desired the jailer to let him have such things as were needful, and he would pay for them. He would not leave the poor fellow till he had given him, with his own hands, some broth which the jailer had got ready for him, and some medicines which the doctor had sent. All this kindness cut Brown to the heart. He was just able to sob out, "My unnatural father leaves me to perish, and my injured friend is more than a father to me." Stock told him that one proof he must give of his repentance was, that he must forgive his father whose provocation had been very great. He then said he would leave him for the present to take some rest, and desired him to lift up his heart to God for mercy. "Dear James," replied Brown, "do you pray for me. God perhaps may hear you, but he will never hear the prayer of such a sinner as I have been." "Take care how you think so," said Stock. "To believe that God can not forgive you, would be still a greater sin than any you have yet committed against him." He then explained to him in a few words, as well as he was able, the nature of repentance and forgiveness through a Savior, and warned him earnestly against unbelief and hardness of heart.

Poor Jack grew much refreshed in body with the comfortable things he had taken, and a little cheered with Stock's kindness in coming so far to see and to forgive such a forlorn outcast, sick of an infectious distemper, and locked within the walls of a prison.

"Surely," said he to himself, "there must be some mighty power in a religion which can lead men to do such things! things so much against the grain as to forgive such an injury, and to risk catching such a distemper;" but he was so weak, he could not express this in words. He tried to pray, but he could not; at length, overpowered with weariness, he fell asleep.

When Mr. Stock came back, he was surprised to find him so much better in body ; but his agonies of mind were dreadful, and he had now got strength to express part of the horrors which he felt. "James," said he, looking wildly, "it is all over with me. I am a lost creature. Even your prayers can not save me." "Dear Jack," replied Mr. Stock, "I am no minister; it does not become me to talk much to thee ; but I know I may venture to say whatever is in the Bible. As ignorant as I am, I shall be safe enough while I stick to that."—"Ay," said the sick man, "you used to be ready enough to read to me, and I would not listen, or if I did it was only to make fun of what I heard, and now you will not so much as read a bit of a chapter to me."

This was the very point to which Stock longed to bring him. So he took a little Bible out of his pocket.

which he always carried with him on a journey, and read slowly, verse by verse, the fifty-fifth chapter of Isaiah. When he came to the sixth and seventh verses, poor Jack cried so much that Stock was forced to stop. The words were, *Let the wicked man forsake his way, and the unrighteous man his thoughts, and let him return unto the Lord.* Here Brown stopped him saying, " Oh, it is too late, too late for me."— " Let me finish the verse," said Stock, " and you will see your error; you will see that it is never too late." So he read on—*Let him return unto the Lord, and he will have mercy upon him, and to our God, and he will abundantly pardon.* Here Brown started up, snatched the book out of his hand, and cried out, " Is that really there? No, no; that's of your own putting in, in order to comfort me; let me look at the words myself."—" No, indeed," said Stock, " I would not for the world give you unfounded comfort, or put off any notion of my own for a Scripture doctrine."—" But is it possible," cried the sick man, " that God may really pardon me? Dost think he can? Dost think he will?"—" I dare not give thee false hopes, or indeed any hopes of my own. But these are God's own words, and the only difficulty is to know when we are really brought into such a state as that the words may be applied to us; for a text may be full of comfort, and yet may not belong to us."

Mr. Stock was afraid of saying more. He would not venture out of his depth; nor indeed was poor Brown able to bear more discourse just now. So he made him a present of the Bible, folding down such places as he thought might be best suited to his state, and took his leave, being obliged to return home that night. He left a little money with the jailer, to add a few comforts to the allowance of the prison, and promised to return in a short time.

When he got home, he described the sufferings and misery of Brown in a very moving manner;-but Tommy Williams, instead of being properly affected by it, only said, "Indeed, master, I am not very sorry; he is rightly served."—"How, Tommy," said Mr. Stock, rather sternly, "not sorry to see a fellow-creature brought to the lowest state of misery, one too whom you have known so prosperous?" "No, master, I can't say I am ; for Mr. Brown used to make fun of you, and laugh at you for being so godly, and reading your Bible."

"Let me say a few words to you Tommy," said Mr. Stock. "In the first place you should never watch for the time of a man's being brought low by trouble to tell of his faults. Next, you should never rejoice at his trouble, but pity him, and pray for him. Lastly, as to his ridiculing me for my religion, if I can not stand an idle jest, I am not worthy the name of a Christian. *He that is ashamed of me and my word*—dost remember what follows, Tommy?"— " Yes, master, it was last Sunday's text—*of him shall the Son of Man be ashamed when he shall judge the world.*"

Mr. Stock soon went back to the prison. But he did not go alone. He took with him Mr. Thomas, the worthy minister who had been the guide and in-structer of his youth, who was so kind as to go at his request and visit this forlorn prisoner. When they got to Brown's door, they found him sitting up in his bed with the Bible in his hand. This was a joyful sight to Mr. Stock, who secretly thanked God for it. Brown was reading aloud; they listened ; it was the fifteenth of Saint Luke. The circumstances of this beautiful parable of the prodigal son were so much like his own, that the story pierced him to the soul ; and he stopped every minute to compare his own case with that of the prodigal. He was just got to the eighteenth verse, *I will arise and go to my father* —at that moment he spied his two friends; joy darted into his eyes. "O dear Jem," said he, " it is *not* too late. I will arise and go to my Father, my heavenly Father, and you, sir, will show me the way, won' you?" said he to Mr. Thomas, whom he recollected. "I am very glad to see you in so hopeful a disposition," said the good minister. "O, sir," said Brown, "what a place is this to receive you in? O, see to what I have brought myself!"

"Your condition, as to this world, is indeed very low," replied the good divine. "But what are mines, dungeons, or galleys, to that eternal hopeless prison to which your unrepented sins must soon have consigned you. Even in this gloomy prison, on this bed of straw, worn down by pain, poverty, and want, forsaken by your worldly friends, an object of scorn to those with whom you used to carouse and riot; yet here, I say, brought thus low, if you have at last found out your own vileness, and your utterly undone state by sin, you may still be more an object of favor in the sight of God, than when you thought yourself prosperous and happy; when the world smiled upon you, and you passed your days and nights in envied gayety and unchristian riot. If you will but improve the present awful visitation; if you do but heartily renounce and abhor your present evil courses; if you even now turn to the Lord your Savior with lively faith, deep repentance, and unfeigned obedience, I shall still have more hope of you than of many who are going on quite happy, because quite insensible. The heavy laden sinner, who has discovered the iniquity of his own heart, and his utter inability to help himself, may be restored to God's favor, and become happy, though in a dungeon. And be assured, that he who from deep and humble contrition dares not so much as lift up his eyes to heaven, when with a hearty faith he sighs out, *Lord be merciful to me a sinner*, shall in no wise be cast out. These are the words of Him who can not lie."

It is impossible to describe the self-abasement, the grief, the joy, the shame, the hope, and the fear, which filled the mind of this poor man. A dawn of comfort at length shone on his benighted mind. His humility and fear of falling back into his former sins, if he should ever recover, Mr. Thomas thought were strong symptoms of a sound repentance. He improved and cherished every good disposition he saw arising in his heart, and particularly warned him against self-deceit, self-confidence, and hypocrisy.

After Brown had deeply expressed his sorrow for his offences, Mr. Thomas thus addressed him. "There are two ways of being sorry for sin. Are you, Mr. Brown, afraid of the guilt of sin because of the punishment annexed to it, or are you afraid of sin itself? Do you wish to be delivered from the power of sin? Do you hate sin because you know it is offensive to a pure and holy God? Or are you only ashamed of it because it has brought you to a prison and exposed you to the contempt of the world? It is not said that the wages of this or that particular sin is death, but of sin in general; there is no exception made because it is a more creditable or a favorite sin, or because it is a little one. There are, I repeat, two ways of being sorry for sin. Cain was sorry— *My punishment is greater than I can bear*, said he; but here you see the punishment seemed to be the cause of concern, not the sin. David seems to have had a good notion of godly sorrow, when he says, *Wash me from mine iniquity, cleanse me from my sin.* And when Job *repented in dust and ashes*, it is not said he excused himself, but he *abhorred himself*. And the prophet Isaiah called himself undone, because he was *a man of unclean lips*; for, said he 'I have seen the King, the Lord of hosts;' that is, he could not take the proper measure of his own iniquity till he had considered the perfect holiness of God."

One day, when Mr. Thomas and Mr. Stock came to see him, they found him more than commonly affected. His face was more ghastly pale than usual, and his eyes were red with crying. "Oh, sir," said he, "what a sight have I just seen! jolly George, as we used to call him, the ringleader of all our mirth.

who was at the bottom of all the fun and tricks, and
wickedness that are carried on within these walls,
jolly George is just dead of the jail distemper! He
taken, and I left! I *would* be carried into his room
to speak to him, to beg him to take warning by me,
and that I might take warning by him. But what
did I see! what did I hear! not one sign of repentance; not one dawn of hope. Agony of body, blas-
phemies on his tongue, despair in his soul; while I
am spared and comforted with hopes of mercy and
acceptance. Oh, if all my old friends at the Grayhound could but then have seen jolly George! A
hundred sermons about death, sir, don't speak so
home, and cut so deep, as the sight of one dying
sinner."

Brown grew gradually better in his health, that is,
the fever mended, but the distemper settled in his
limbs, so that he seemed likely to be a poor, weakly
cripple the rest of his life. But as he spent much of
his time in prayer, and in reading such parts of the
Bible as Mr. Thomas directed, he improved every day
in knowledge and piety, and of course grew more
resigned to pain and infirmity.

Some months after this, his hard-hearted father,
who had never been prevailed upon to see him, or
offer him the least relief, was taken off suddenly by a
fit of apoplexy; and, after all his threatenings, he
died without a will. He was one of those silly, su
perstitious men, who fancy they shall die the sooner
for having made one; and who love the world and
the things that are in the world so dearly, that they
dread to set about any business which may put them
in mind that they are not always to live in it. As by
this neglect, his father had not fulfilled his threat of
cutting him off with a shilling, Jack, of course, went
shares with his brothers in what their father left.
What fell to him proved to be just enough to discharge him from prison, and to pay all his debts, but
he had nothing left. His joy at being thus enabled

11

to make restitution was so great that he thought little
of his own wants. He did not desire to conceal the
most trifling debt, nor to keep a shilling for himself.

Mr. Stock undertook to settle all his affairs. There
did not remain money enough after every creditor
was satisfied, even to pay for his removal home. Mr
Stock kindly sent his own cart for him with a bed in
it, made as comfortable as possible, for he was too
weak and lame to be removed any other way, and
Mrs. Stock gave the driver particular charge to be
tender and careful of him, and not to drive hard, nor
to leave the cart a moment.

Mr. Stock would fain have taken him into his own
house, at least for a time, so convinced was he of the
sincere reformation both of heart and life ; but Brown
would not be prevailed on to be further burdensome
to this generous friend. He insisted on being carried
to the parish workhouse, which he said was a far
better place than he deserved. In this house Mr.
Stock furnished a small room for him, and sent him
every day a morsel of meat from his own dinner.
Tommy Williams begged that he might always be
allowed to carry it, as some atonement for his having
for a moment so far forgotten his duty, as rather to rejoice than sympathize in Brown's misfortunes. He
never thought of this fault without sorrow, and often
thanked his master for the wholesome lesson he
then gave him, and he was the better for it all his life.

Mr. Stock often carried poor Brown a dish of tea
or a basin of good broth herself. He was quite a
cripple, and never able to walk out as long as he
lived. Mr. Stock, Will Simpson, and Tommy Williams, laid their heads together, and contrived a sort
of barrow on which he was often carried to church
by some of his poor neighbors, of which Tommy
was always one ; and he requited their kindness by
reading a good book to them whenever they would
call in ; and he spent his time in teaching their children to sing psalms or say the catechism.

It was no small joy to him thus to be enabled to go o church. Whenever he was carried by the Grayhound, he was much moved, and used to put up a prayer full of repentance for the past, and praise for the present.

Dialogue between James Stock and Will Simpson, the shoemakers, on the duty of carrying religion into our common business.

JAMES STOCK and his journeyman, Will Simpson, having resolved to work together one hour every evening, in order to pay for Tommy Williams's schooling; this circumstance brought them to be a good deal together when the rest of the men were gone home. Now it happened that Mr. Stock had a pleasant way of endeavoring to turn all common events to some use; and he thought it right on the present occasion to make the only return in his power to Will Simpson for his great kindness. For, said he, if Will gives up so much of his time to help to provide for this poor boy, it is the least I can do to try to turn part of that time to the purpose of promoting Will's spiritual good. Now as the bent of Stock's own mind was religious, it was easy to him to lead their talk to something profitable. He always took especial care, however, that the subject should be introduced properly, cheerfully, and without constraint. As he well knew that great good may be sometimes done by a prudent attention in seizing proper opportunities, so he knew that the cause of piety had been sometimes hurt by forcing serious subjects where there was clearly no disposition to receive them. I say he had found out that two things were necessary to the promoting of religion among his friends; a warm zeal to be always on the watch for occasions, and a cool judgment to distinguish which was the right time and place to make use of them. To know *how* to do good is a great matter, but to know *when* to do it is no small one.

Simpson was an honest, good-natured young man, he was now become sober, and rather religiously disposed. But he was ignorant—he did not know much of the grounds of religion, or of the corruption of his own nature. He was regular at church, but was first drawn thither rather by his skill in psalm-singing than by any great devotion. He had left off going to the Grayhound, and often read the Bible, or some other good book on the Sunday evening. This he thought was quite enough; he thought the Bible was the prettiest history-book in the world, and that religion was a very good thing for Sundays. But he did not much understand what business people had with it on working-days. He had left off drinking because it had brought Williams to the grave, and his wife to dirt and rags, but not because he himself had seen the evil of sin. He now considered swearing and sabbath-breaking as scandalous and indecent, but he had not found out that both were to be left off because they are highly offensive to God, and grieve his Holy Spirit. As Simpson was less self-conceited than most ignorant people are, Stock had always a good hope that when he should come to be better acquainted with the word of God, and with the evil of his own heart, he would become one day a good Christian. The great hinderance to this was, that he fancied himself so already.

One evening Simpson had been calling to Stock's mind how disorderly the house and shop, where they were now sitting quietly at work, had formerly been, and he went on thus:

Will. How comfortably we live now, master, to what we used to do in Williams's time! I used then never to be happy but when we were keeping it up all night, but now I am as merry as the day is long. I find I am twice as happy since I am grown good and sober.

Stock. I am glad you are happy, Will, and I rejoice that you are sober; but I would not have you take too much pride in your own *goodness*, for fear it should become a sin, almost as great as some of those you have left off. Besides, I would not have you make quite so sure that you *are* good.

Will. Not good, master! why, don't you find me regular and orderly at work?

Stock. Very much so, and accordingly I have a great respect for you.

Will. I pay every one his own, seldom miss church, have not been drunk since Williams died, have handsome clothes for Sundays, and save a trifle every week.

Stock. Very true, and very laudable it is; and to all this you may add that you very generously work an hour for poor Tommy's education every evening, without fee or reward.

Will. Well, master, what can a man do more? If all this is not being good, I don't know what is.

Stock. All these things are very right as far as they go, and you could not well be a Christian without doing them. But I shall make you stare, perhaps, when I tell you you may do all these things, and many more, and yet be no Christian.

Will. No Christian! surely, master, I do hope that after all I have done you will not be so unkind as to say I am no Christian.

Stock. God forbid that I should say so, Will. I hope better things of you. But come now, what do you think it is to be a Christian?

Will. What! why, to be christened when one is a child; to learn the catechism when one can read; to be confirmed when one is a youth, and to go to church when one is a man.

Stock. These are all very proper things, and quite necessary. They make part of a Christian's life. But for all that a man may be exact in them all, and yet not be a Christian.

Will. Not be a Christian! ha! ha! ha! you are very comical, master.

Stock. No, indeed, I am very serious, Will. At this rate it would be a very easy thing to be a Christian, and every man who went through certain forms would be a good man, and one man who observed those forms would be as good as another. Whereas, if we come to examine ourselves by the word of God, I am afraid there are but few comparatively whom our Savior would allow to be real Christians. What is your notion of a Christian's practice?

Will. Why, he must not rob, nor murder, nor get drunk. He must avoid scandalous things, and do as other decent, orderly people do.

Stock. It is easy enough to be what the world calls a Christian, but not to be what the Bible calls so.

Will. Why, master, we working-men are not expected to be saints, and martyrs, and apostles, and ministers.

Stock. We are not. And yet, Will, there are not two sorts of Christianity; we are called to practise the same religion which they practised, and something of the same spirit is expected in us which we reverence in them. It was not saints and martyrs only to whom our Savior said that they must *crucify the world with its affections and lusts.* We are called to *be holy* in our measure and degree. *as he who hath called us is holy.* It was not only saints and martyrs who were told that they must be *like minded with Christ.* That *they must do all to the glory of God.* That *they must renounce the spirit of the world, and deny themselves.* It was not to apostles only that Christ said, *They must have their conversation in heaven.* It was not to a few holy men, set apart for the altar, that he said, *They must set their affections on things above.* That *they must not be conformed to the world.* No; it was to fishermen, to publicans, to farmers, to day-laborers, to poor tradesmen, that he spoke when he told them they must *love not the world, nor the things of the world.* That *they must renounce the hidden things of dishonesty, grow in grace, lay up for themselves treasures in heaven.*

Will. All this might be very proper for *them* to be taught, because they had not been bred up Christians, but Heathens or Jews, and Christ wanted to make them his followers, that is, Christians. But, thank God, we do not want to be taught all this, for we *are* Christians, born in a Christian country, of Christian parents.

Stock. I suppose, then, you fancy that Christianity comes to people in a Christian country by nature.

Will. I think it comes by a good education or a good example. When a fellow who has got any sense sees a man cut off in his prime by drinking, like Williams, I think he will begin to leave it off. When he sees another man respected, like you, master, for honesty and sobriety, and going to church, why, he will grow honest, and sober, and go to church, that is, he will see it his advantage to be a Christian.

Stock. Will, what you say is the truth, but 'tis not the whole truth. You are right as far as you go, but you do not go far enough. The worldly advantages of piety, are, as you suppose, in general great. Credit, prosperity, and health, almost naturally attend on a religious life, both because a religious life supposes a sober and industrious life, and because a man who lives in a course of duty puts himself in the way of God's blessing. But a true Christian has a still higher aim in view, and will follow religion even under circumstances when it may hurt his credit and ruin his prosperity if it should ever happen to be the will of God that he should be brought into such a trying state.

Will. Well, master, to speak the truth, if I go to church on Sundays, and follow my work in the week, I must say I think that is being good.

Stock. I agree with you, that he who does both, gives the best outward signs that he is good, as you

call it. But our going to church, and even reading
the Bible, are no proofs that we are as good as we
need be, but rather that we do both these in order to
make us better than we are. We do both on Sundays, as means, by God's blessing, to make us better
all the week. We are to bring the fruits of that
chapter or of that sermon into our daily life, and try
to get our inmost heart and secret thoughts as well
as our daily conduct amended by them.

Will. Why, sure, master, you won't be so unrea-
sonable as to want a body to be religious always. I
can't do that neither. I'm not such a hypocrite as to
pretend to it.

Stock. Yes, you can be so in every action of your
life.

Will. What, master, always to be thinking about
religion ?

Stock. No, far from it, Will, much less to be always talking about it. But you must be always under its power and spirit.

Will. But surely 'tis pretty well if I do this when
I go to church, or while I am saying my prayers.
Even you, master, as strict as you are, would not
have me always on my knees, nor always at church,
I suppose, for then how would your work be carried
on, and how would our town be supplied with shoes?

Stock. Very true, Will. 'Twould be no proof of
our religion to let our customers go barefoot, but
'twould be a proof of our laziness, and we should
starve, as we ought to do. The business of the
world must not only be carried on, but carried on
with spirit and activity. We have the same authority
for not being *slothful in business*, as we have for being
fervent in spirit. Religion has put godliness and laziness as wide asunder as any two things in the world,
and what God has separated let no man pretend to
join. Indeed, the spirit of religion can have no fellowship with sloth, indolence, and self-indulgence.
But still, a Christian does not carry on his common

trade quite like another man neither, for something of the spirit which he labors to attain at church, he carries with him into his worldly concerns. While there are some who set up for Sunday Christians, who have no notion that they are bound to be week-day Christians too.

Will. Why, master, I do think, if God Almighty is contented with one day in seven, he won't thank you for throwing him the other six into the bargain. I thought he gave us them for our own use, and I am sure nobody works harder all the week than you do.

Stock. God, it is true, sets apart one day in seven for actual rest from labor, and for more immediate devotion to his service. But show me that text wherein he says, Thou shalt love the Lord thy God on *Sundays*—Thou shalt keep my commandments on the *sabbath-day*—To be carnally-minded on *Sundays is death*—Cease to do evil, and learn to do well *one day* in *seven*—Grow in grace on the *Lord's day*—Is there any such text?

Will. No, to be sure there is not, for that would be encouraging sin on all the other days.

Stock. Yes, just as you do when you make religion a thing for the church and not for the world. There is no one lawful calling, in pursuing which we may not serve God acceptably. You and I may serve him while we are stitching this pair of boots. Farmer Furrow while he is ploughing yonder field. Betsy West, over-the-way, while she is nursing her sick mother. Neighbor Incle, in measuring out his tapes and ribands. I say all these may serve God just as acceptably in those employments as at church—I had almost said more so.

Will. Ay, indeed; how can that be? Now you're too much on t'other side.

Stock. Because a man's trials in trade being often greater, they give him fresh means of glorifying God and proving the sincerity of religion. A man who mixes in business is naturally brought into continua temptations and difficulties. These will lead him, if he be a good man, to look more to God than he perhaps would otherwise do. He sees temptations on the right hand and on the left; he knows that there are snares all around him; this makes him watchful; he feels that the enemy within is too ready to betray him; this makes him humble himself, while a sense of his own difficulties makes him tender to the failings of others.

Will. Then you would make one believe, after all, that trade and business must be sinful in itself, since it brings a man into all these snares and scrapes.

Stock. No, no, Will; trade and business don't create evil passions—they were in the heart before—only now and then they seem to lie snug a little—our concerns with the world bring them out into action a little more, and thus show both others and ourselves what we really are. But then, as the world offers more trials on the one hand, so on the other it holds out more duties. If we are called to battle oftener, we have more opportunities of victory. Every temptation resisted is an enemy subdued, and *he that ruleth his own spirit, is better than he that taketh a city.*

Will. I don't quite understand you, master.

Stock. I will try to explain myself. There is no passion more called out by the transactions of trade than covetousness. Now, 'tis impossible to withstand such a master sin as that, without carrying a good deal of the spirit of religion into one's trade.

Will. Well, I own I don't yet see how I am to be religious when I'm hard at work, or busy settling an account. I can't do two things at once; 'tis as if I were to pretend to make a shoe and cut out a boot at the same moment.

Stock. I tell you both must subsist together. Nay, the one must be the motive to the other. God commands us to be industrious, and if we love him, the desire of pleasing him should be the main spring of our industry.

Will. I don't see how I can always be thinking about pleasing God.

Stock. Suppose, now, a man had a wife and children whom he loved, and wished to serve; would he not be often thinking about them while he was at work? and though he would not be *always* thinking nor always talking about them, yet would not the very love he bore them be a constant spur to his industry? He would always be pursuing the same course from the same motive, though his words and even his thoughts must often be taken up in the common transactions of life.

Will. I say first one, then the other; now for labor, now for religion.

Stock. I will show that both must go together. I will suppose you were going to buy so many skins of our currier; that is quite a business transaction; you can't see what a spirit of religion has to do with a few calfskins. Now, I tell you it has a great deal to do with it. Covetousness, a desire to make a good bargain, may rise up in your heart. Selfishness, a spirit of monopoly, a wish to get all, in order to distress others; these are evil desires, and must be subdued. Some opportunity of unfair gain offers, in which there may be much sin, and yet little scandal. Here a Christian will stop short; he will recollect, *That he who maketh haste to be rich shall hardly be innocent.* Perhaps the sin may be on the side of your dealer—*he* may want to overreach *you*—this is provoking—you are tempted to violent anger, perhaps to swear;—here is a fresh demand on you for a spirit of patience and moderation, as there was before for a spirit of justice and self-denial. If, by God's grace, you get the victory over these temptations, you are the better man for having been called out to them, always provided, that the temptations be not of your own seeking. If you give way, and sink under these temptations, don't go and say trade and business have made you covetous, passionate, and profane. No, no; depend upon it, you were so before; you would have had all these evil seeds lurking in your heart, if you had been loitering about at home and doing nothing, with the additional sin of idleness into the bargain. When you are busy, the devil often tempts you; when you are idle, you tempt the devil. If business and the world call these evil tempers into action, business and the world call that religion into action too which teaches us to resist them. And in this you see the week-day fruit of the Sunday's piety. 'Tis trade and business in the week which call us to put our Sunday readings, praying, and church-going, into practice.

Will. Well, master, you have a comical way, somehow, of coming over one. I never should have thought there would have been any religion wanted in buying and selling a few calfskins. But I begin to see there is a good deal in what you say. And, whenever I am doing a common action, I will try to remember that it must be done *after a godly sort.*

Stock. I hear the clock strike nine—let us leave off our work. I will only observe farther, that one good end of our bringing religion into our business is, to put us in mind not to undertake more business than we can carry on consistently with our religion. I shall never commend that man's diligence, though it is often commended by the world, who is not diligent about the salvation of his soul. We are as much forbidden to be overcharged with the *cares* of life, as with its *pleasures.* I only wish to prove to you, that a discreet Christian may be wise for both worlds; that he may employ his hands without entangling his soul, and labor for the meat that perisheth, without neglecting that which endureth unto eternal life; that he may be prudent for time while he is wise for eternity.

The duty of carrying religion into our amusements.

The next evening, Will Simpson being got first to his work, Mr. Stock found him singing very cheerfully over his last. His master's entrance did not prevent his finishing his song, which concluded with these words :—

" Since life is no more than a passage at best,
    Let us strew the way over with flowers."

When Will had concluded his song, he turned to Mr. Stock, and said, " I thank you, master, for first putting it into my head how wicked it is to sing profane and indecent songs. I never sing any now which have any wicked words in them."

Stock. I am glad to hear it. So far you do well. But there are other things as bad as wicked words, nay, worse perhaps, though they do not so much shock the ear of decency.

Will. What is that, master ? What can be so bad as wicked words ?

Stock. Wicked *thoughts*, Will ; which thoughts, when they are covered over with smooth words, and dressed out in pleasing rhymes, so as not to shock modest young people by the sound, do more harm to their principles than those songs of which the words are so gross and disgusting, that no person of common decency can for a moment listen to them.

Will. Well, master, I am sure that was a very pretty song I was singing when you came in, and a song which very sober good people sing.

Stock. Do they ? Then I will be bold to say, that singing such songs is no part of their goodness. 1 heard indeed but two lines of it, but they were so heathenish that I desire to hear no more.

Will. Now you are really too hard. What harm could there be in it ? there was not one indecent word.

Stock. I own, indeed, that indecent words are particularly offensive. But, as I said before, though im-

12

modest expressions offend the ear more, they do not
corrupt the heart, perhaps, much more than songs of
which the words are decent, and the principle vicious.
In the latter case, because there is nothing that shocks
his ear, a man listens till the sentiment has so corrupted his heart, that his ears grow hardened too, and
by long custom he loses all sense of the danger of profane diversions; and I must say I have often heard
young women of character sing songs in company,
which I should be ashamed to read by myself. But
come, as we work, let us talk over this business a
little; and first let us stick to this sober song of yours,
that you boast so much about.   (*repeats.*)

> " Since life is no more than a passage at best,
>   Let us strew the way over with flowers."

Now, what do you learn by this?

Will. Why, master, I don't pretend to learn much
by it. But 'tis a pretty tune and pretty words.

Stock. But what do these pretty words mean?

Will. That we must make ourselves merry because
life is short.

Stock. Will! of what religion are you?

Will. You are always asking one such odd questions, master; why, a Christian, to be sure.

Stock. If I often ask you, or others this question,
it is only because I like to know what grounds I am
to go upon when I am talking with you or them. I
conceive that there are in this country two sorts of
people, Christians and no Christians. Now, if people
profess to be of this first description, I expect one
kind of notions, opinions, and behavior, from them: if
they say they are of the latter, then I look for another
set of notions and actions from them. I compel no
man to think with me. I take every man at his
word. I only expect him to think and believe according to the character he takes upon himself, and
to act on the principles of that character which he
professes to maintain.

Will. That's fair enough ; I can't say but it is, to take a man at his own word, and on his own grounds.

Stock. Well, then. Of whom does the Scripture speak when it says, *Let us eat and drink, for to-morrow we die ?*

Will. Why of heathens, to be sure, not of Christians.

Stock. And of whom when it says, *Let us crown ourselves with rosebuds before they are withered ?*

Will. O, that is Solomon's worldly fool.

Stock. You disapprove of both, then.

Will. To be sure I do. I should not be a Christian if I did not.

Stock. And yet, though a Christian, you are admiring the very same thought in the song you were singing. How do you reconcile this ?

Will. O, there is no comparison between them. These several texts are designed to describe loose, wicked heathens. Now I learn texts as a part of my religion. But religion, you know, has nothing to do with a song. I sing a song for my pleasure.

Stock. In our last night's talk, Will, I endeavored to prove to you that religion was to be brought into our *business.* I wish now to let you see that it is to be brought into our *pleasure* also ; and that he who is really a Christian, must be a Christian in his very diversions.

Will. Now you are too strict again, master, as you last night declared, that in our business you would not have us always praying, so I hope that in our pleasure you would not have us always psalm-singing. I hope you would not have all one's singing to be about good things.

Stock. Not so, Will; but I would not have any part, either of our business or our pleasure, to be about evil things. It is one thing to be singing *about* religion, it is another thing to be singing *against* it. St. Peter, I fancy, would not much have approved your favorite song. He at least seemed to have another view of the matter, when he said, *The end of all things is at hand.* Now this text teaches much the same awful truth with the first line of your song. But let us see to what different purposes the apostle and the poet turn the very same thought. Your song says, "because life is short, let us make it merry. Let us divert ourselves so much on the road, that we may forget the end." Now what says the apostle: *Because the end of all things is at hand, be ye therefore sober and watch unto prayer.*

Will. Why, master, I like to be sober too, and have left off drinking. But still I never thought that we were obliged to carry texts out of the Bible to try the soundness of a song, and to enable us to judge if we might be both merry and wise in singing it.

Stock. Providence has not so stinted our enjoyments, Will, but he has left us many subjects of harmless merriment: but, for my own part, I am never certain that any one is quite harmless till I have tried it by this rule that you seem to think so strict. As I passed by the Grayhound last night, in my way to my evening's walk in the fields, I caught this one verse of a song which the club were singing :—

> " Bring the flask, the music bring,
>   Joy shall quickly find us ;
> Drink and dance, and laugh and sing,
>   And cast dull care behind us."

When I got into the fields, I could not forbear comparing this song with the words: *Take heed lest at any time your heart be overcharged with drunkenness, and so that day come upon you unawares, for as a snare shall it come upon all them that are on the face of the earth.*

Will. Why, to be sure, if that is right, the song must be wrong.

Stock. I ran over in my mind also a comparison between such songs as that which begins with

> " Drink, and drive care away."

with those injunctions of holy writ, *Watch and pray, therefore, that you enter not into temptation ;* and again, *Watch and pray that you may escape oll these things.* I say I compared this with the song I allude to—

> " Drink, and drive care away,
> Drink and be merry ;
> You'll ne'er go the faster
> To the Stygian ferry."

I compared this with that awful admonition of Scripture how to pass the time : *Not in rioting and drunkenness, not in chambering and wantonness, but put ye on the Lord Jesus Christ, and make not provision for the flesh to fulfil the lusts thereof.*

Will. Master, now you have opened my eyes, I think I can make some of those comparisons myself between the spirit of the Bible and the spirit of these songs.

> " Bring the flask, the goblet bring,"

won't stand very well in company with the threat of the prophet : *Wo unto them that rise up early, that they may mingle strong drink.*

Stock. Ay, Will ; and these thoughtless people who live up to their singing, seem to be the very people described in another place as glorying in their intemperance, and acting what their songs describe :— *They look at the wine, and say it is red, it moveth itself aright in the cup.*

Will. I do hope I shall for the future not only become more careful what songs I sing myself, but also not to keep company with those who sing nothing else but what in my sober judgment I now see to be wrong.

Stock. As we shall have no *body* in the world to come, it is a pity not only to make our pleasures here consist entirely in the delights of animal life, but to make our very songs consist in extolling and exalting those delights which are unworthy of the man as well as of the Christian. If, through temptation or weakness, we fall into errors, let us not establish and confirm them by picking up all the songs and scraps of verses which excuse, justify, and commend sin. That time is short, is a reason given by these song-mongers why we should give into greater indulgences. That time is short, is a reason given by the apostle why we should enjoy our dearest comforts as if we enjoyed them not.

Now, Will, I hope you will see the importance of so managing, that our diversions may be as carefully chosen as our other employments. For to make them such as effectually drive out of our minds all that the Bible and the minister have been putting into them, seems to me as imprudent as it is unchristian. But this is not all. Such sentiments as these songs contain, set off by the prettiest music, heightened by liquor and all the noise and spirit of what is called jovial company, all this, I say, not only puts everything that is right out of the mind, but puts everything that is wrong into it. Such songs, therefore, as tend to promote levity, thoughtlessness, loose imaginations, false views of life, forgetfulness of death, contempt of whatever is serious, and neglect of whatever is sober, whether they be love songs, or drinking songs, will not, can not be sung by any man or any woman who makes a serious profession of Christianity.

IV. GILES THE POACHER;

CONTAINING SOME ACCOUNT OF A FAMILY WHO HAD RATHER LIVE BY THEIR WITS THAN THEIR WORK.

POACHING GILES lives on the borders of those great moors in Somersetshire. Giles, to be sure, has been a sad fellow in his time, and it is none of his fault if his whole family do not end their career either at the gallows or Botany Bay. He lives at that mud cottage with the broken windows, stuffed with dirty rags, just beyond the gate which divides the upper from the lower moor. You may know the house at a good distance by the ragged tiles on the roof, and the loose stones which are ready to drop out from the chimney, though a short ladder, a hod of mortar, and half an hour's leisure time would have prevented all this, and made the little dwelling tight enough. But as Giles had never learned anything that was good, so he did not know the value of such useful sayings, as that "a tile in time saves nine."

Besides this, Giles fell into that common mistake, that a beggarly-looking cottage, and filthy, ragged children, raised most compassion, and of course drew most charity. But as cunning as he was in other things, he was out in his reckoning here, for it is neatness, housewifery, and a decent appearance, which draw the kindness of the rich and charitable, while they turn away disgusted from filth and laziness, not out of pride, but because they see that it is next to impossible to mend the condition of those who de grade themselves by dirt and sloth; and few people care to help those who will not help themselves.

The common on which Giles's hovel stands, is quite a deep marsh in a wet winter, but in summer it looks green and pretty enough. To be sure it would be rather convenient when one passes that way in a carriage, if one of the children would run out and open the gate, but instead of any one of them running out as soon as they heard the wheels, which would be quite time enough, what does Giles do, but set all his ragged brats, with dirty faces, matted locks, and naked feet and legs, to lie all day upon a sand-bank hard by the gate, waiting for the slender chance of what may be picked up from travellers. At the sound of a carriage, a whole covey of these little scare-crows start up, rush to the gate, and all at once thrust out their hats and aprons, and for fear this, together with the noise of their clamorous begging, should not sufficiently frighten the horses, they are very apt to let the gate slap full against you, before you are half way through, in their eager scuffle to snatch from each other the half-pence which you have thrown out to them. I know two ladies who were one day very near being killed by these abominable tricks.

Thus five or six little idle creatures, who might be earning a trifle by knitting at home, who might be useful to the public by working in the field, and who might assist their families by learning to get their bread twenty honest ways, are suffered to lie about all day, in the hope of a few chance half-pence, which after all, they are by no means sure of getting. Indeed, when the neighboring gentlemen found out that opening the gate was a family trade, they soon left off giving anything. And I myself, though I used to take out a penny ready to give, had there been only one to receive it, when I see a whole family established in so beggarly a trade, quietly put it back again in my pocket, and give nothing at all.

And so few travellers pass that way, that sometimes after the whole family have lost a day, their gains do not amount to two-pence.

As Giles had a far greater taste for living by his wits than his work, he was at one time in hopes that his children might have got a pretty penny by *tumbling* for the diversion of travellers, and he set about training them in that indecent practice, but unluckily the moors being level, the carriage travelled faster than the children tumbled. He envied those parents who lived on the London road, over the Wiltshire downs, which downs being very hilly, it enables the tumbles to keep pace with the traveller, till he sometimes extorts from the light and unthinking a reward instead of a reproof. I beg leave, however, to put all gentlemen and ladies in mind, that such tricks are a kind of apprenticeship to the trades of begging and thieving, and that nothing is more injurious to good morals than to encourage the poor in any habits which may lead them to live upon chance.

Giles, to be sure, as his children grew older, began to train them to such other employments as the idle habits they had learned at the gate very properly qualified them for. The right of common, which some of the poor cottagers have in that part of the country, and which is doubtless a considerable advantage to many, was converted by Giles into the means of corrupting his whole family, for his children, as soon as they grew too big·for the trade of begging at the gate, were promoted to the dignity of thieves on the moor. Here he kept two or three asses, miserable beings, which if they had the good fortune to escape an untimely death by starving, did not fail to meet with it by beating. Some of the biggest boys were sent out with these lean and galled animals to carry sand or coals about the neighboring towns. Both sand and coals were often stolen before they got them to sell, or if not, they always took care cheat in selling them. By long practice in this art

they grew so dexterous, that they could give a pretty
good guess how large a coal they could crib out of
every bag before the buyer would be likely to miss it.

All their odd time was taken up under the pretence
of watching their asses on the moor, or running after
five or six half-starved geese, but the truth is, these
boys were only watching for an opportunity to steal
an odd goose of their neighbor's, while they pretended to look after their own. They used also to pluck
the quills or the down from these poor live creatures,
or half milk a cow before the farmer's maid came
with her pail. They all knew how to calculate to a
minute what time to be down in a morning to let out
their lank hungry beasts, which they had turned over
night into the farmer's field to steal a little good pas-
ture. They contrived to get there just time enough
to escape being caught replacing the stakes they had
pulled out for the cattle to get over. For Giles was
a prudent, long-headed fellow, and whenever he stole
food for his colts, took care never to steal stakes from
the hedges at the same place. He had sense enough
to know that the gain did not make up for the danger;
he knew that a loose fagot. pulled from a neighbor's
pile of wood after the family were gone to bed, answered the end better, and was not half the trouble.

Among the many trades which Giles professed, he
sometimes practised that of a rat-eatcher; but he was
addicted to so many tricks, that he never followed the
same trade long, for detection will, sooner or later,
follow the best concerted villany. Whenever he was
sent for to a farm-house, his custom was to kill a few of
the old rats, always taking care to leave a little stock
of young ones alive, sufficient to keep up the breed:
"for," said he, "if I were to be such a fool as to clear
a house or a barn at once. how would my trade be
carried on?" And where any barn was over-stocked
he used to borrow a few rats thence, just to people a neighboring granary which had none ; and he
might have gone on till now, had he not unluckily

been caught one evening emptying his cage of rats under Parson Wilson's barn door.

This worthy minister, Mr. Wilson, used to pity the neglected children of Giles as much as he blamed the wicked parents. He one day picked up Dick, who was far the best of Giles's bad boys. Dick was loitering about in a field behind the parson's garden, in search of a hen's nest, his mother having ordered him to bring home a few eggs that night, by hook or by crook, as Giles was resolved to have some pancakes for supper, though he knew that eggs were a penny a-piece. Mr. Wilson had long been desirous of snatching some of this vagrant family from ruin, and his chief hopes were bent on Dick, as the least hackneyed in knavery. He had once given him a pair of new shoes, on his promising to go to school next Sunday, but no sooner had Rachel, the boy's mother, got the shoes into her clutches, than she pawned them for a bottle of gin, and ordered the boy to keep out of the parson's sight, and to be sure to play his marbles on Sunday, for the future, at the other end of the parish, and not near the churchyard. Mr. Wilson, however, picked up the boy once more, for it was not his way to despair of anybody. Dick was just going to take to his heels, as usual, for fear the old story of the shoes should be brought forward, but finding he could not get off, what does he do but run into a little puddle of muddy water which lay between him and the parson, that the sight of his naked feet might not bring on the dreaded subject. Now it happened that Mr. Wilson was planting a little field of beans, so he thought this a good opportunity to employ Dick, and he told him he had got some pretty easy work for him. Dick did as he was bid: he willingly went to work, and readily began to plant his beans with despatch and regularity according to the directions given him.

While the boy was busily at work by himself, Giles happened to come by, having been skulking

round the back way to look over the parson's garden
wall, to see if there was anything worth climbing
over for on the ensuing night. He spied Dick, and
began to scold him for working for the stingy old
parson, for Giles had a natural antipathy to whatever
belonged to the church. "What has he promised
thee a-day?" said he, "little enough, I dare say."
"He is not to pay me by the day," said Dick, "but
says he will give me so much when I have planted
this peck, and so much for the next." "Oh, oh!
that alters the case," said Giles. "One may, indeed,
get a trifle by this sort of work. I hate your regular
day-jobs, where one can't well avoid doing one's work
for one's money. Come, give me a handful of beans,
I will teach thee how to plant when thou art paid for
planting by the peck. All we have to do in that case
is to despatch the work as fast as we can, and get rid
of the beans with all speed; and as to the seed coming
up or not, that is no business of ours; we are paid
for planting not for growing. At the rate thou goest
on thou wouldst not get sixpence to-night. Come
along, bury away." So saying, he took his hatful of
the seed, and where Dick had been ordered to set one
bean, Giles buried a dozen; of course the beans
were soon out. But though the peck was emptied,
the ground was unplanted. But cunning Giles knew
this could not be found out till the time when the
beans might be expected to come up, "and then,
Dick," says he, "the snails and the mice may go
shares in the blame, or we can lay the fault on the
rooks or the blackbirds." So saying, he sent the boy
into the parsonage to receive his pay, taking care to
secure about a quarter of the peck of beans for his
own colt. He put both bag and beans into his own
pocket to carry home, bidding Dick tell Mr. Wilson
that he had planted the beans and lost the bag.

In the meantime Giles's other boys were busy in
emptying the ponds and trout-streams in the neighboring manor. They would steal away the carp and

tench when they were no bigger than gudgeons. By this untimely depredation they plundered the owner of his property without enriching themselves. But the pleasure of mischief was reward enough. These, and a hundred other little thieveries, they committed with such dexterity, that old Tim Crib, whose son was transported last assizes for sheep-stealing, used to be often reproaching his boys that Giles's sons were worth a hundred of such blockheads as he had; for scarce a night passed but Giles had some little comfortable thing for supper which his boys had pilfered in the day, while his undutiful dogs never stole anything worth having. Giles, in the meantime, was busy in his way; but as busy as he was in laying his nets, starting coveys, and training dogs, he always took care that his depredations should not be confined merely to game.

Giles's boys had never seen the inside of a church, since they were christened, and the father thought he knew his own interest better than to force them to it; for church-time was the season of their harvest. Then the hen's nests were searched, a stray duck was clapped under the smock frock, the tools which might have been left by chance in a farm-yard, were picked up, and all the neighboring pigeon-houses were thinned, so that Giles used to boast to tawny Rachel his wife, that Sunday was to them the most profitable day in the week. With her it was certainly the most laborious day, as she always did her washing and ironing on the Sunday morning, it being, as she said, the only leisure day she had, for on the other days she went about the country telling fortunes, and selling dream-books and wicked songs. Neither her husband's nor her children's clothes were ever mended, and if Sunday, her idle day, had not come about once in every week, it is likely they would never have been washed either. You might however see her as you were going to church, smoothing her own rags on her best red cloak, which she always used for her

13

ironing-cloth on Sundays, for her cloak when she travelled, and for her blanket at night; such a wretched manager was Rachel! Among her other articles of trade, one was to make and sell peppermint, and other distilled waters. These she had the cheap art of making without trouble and without expense, for she made them without herbs and without a still. Her way was, to fill so many quart bottles with plain water, putting a spoonful of mint water in the mouth of each : these she corked down with rosin, carrying to each customer a phial of real distilled water to taste by way of sample. This was so good that her bottles were commonly bought up without being opened; but if any suspicion arose, and she was forced to uncork a bottle, by the few drops of distilled water lying at the top, she even then escaped detection, and took care to get out of reach before the bottle was opened a second time. She was too prudent ever to go twice to the same house.

The Upright Magistrate.

There is hardly any petty mischief that is not connected with the life of a poacher. Mr. Wilson was aware of this; he was not only a pious clergyman, but an upright justice. He used to say, that people who were truly conscientious, must be so in small things as well as in great ones, or they would destroy the effect of their own precepts, and their example would not be of general use. For this reason he never would accept of a hare or a partridge from any unqualified person in the parish. He did not content himself with shuffling the thing off by asking questions, and pretending to take it for granted in a general way that the game was fairly come at; but he used to say, that by receiving the booty he connived at a crime, made himself a sharer in it; and if he gave a present to the man who brought it, he even tempted him to repeat the fault.

One day poor Jack Weston, an honest fellow in the

neighborhood, whom Mr. Wilson had kindly visited
and relieved in a long sickness, from which he was
but just recovered, was brought before him as he was
sitting on the justice's bench; Jack was accused of
having knocked down a hare; and of all the birds in
the air who should the informer be but black Giles
the poacher? Mr. Wilson was grieved at the charge;
he had a great regard for Jack, but he had still a
greater regard for the law. The poor fellow pleaded
guilty. He did not deny the fact, but said he did not
consider it as a crime, for he did not think game was
private property, and he owned he had a strong temptation for doing what he had done, which he hoped
would plead his excuse. The justice desired to
know what this temptation was.—"Sir," said the
poor fellow, "You know I was given over this spring
in a bad fever. I had no friend in the world but you,
sir. Under God you saved my life by your charitable
relief; and I trust also you may have helped to save
my soul by your prayers and your good advice; for,
by the grace of God, I have turned over a new leaf
since that sickness.

"I know I can never make you amends for all your
goodness, but I thought it would be some comfort to
my full heart if I could but once give you some little
token of my gratitude. So I had trained a pair of
nice turtle doves for Madam Wilson, but they were
stolen from me, sir, and I do suspect black Giles stole
them. Yesterday morning, sir, as I was crawling out
to my work, for I am still but very weak, a fine hare
ran across my path. I did not stay to consider whether it was wrong to kill a hare, but I felt it was right
to show my gratitude; so, sir, without a moment's
thought I did knock down the hare, which I was going to carry to your worship, because I knew madam
was fond of hare. I am truly sorry for my fault, and
will submit to whatever punishment your worship
may please to inflict."

Mr. Wilson was much moved with this honest

confession, and touched with the poor fellow's grati
tude.   What added to the effect of the story, was the
weak condition and pale sickly looks of the offender
But this worthy magistrate never suffered his feeling
to bias his integrity ; he knew that he did not sit on
that bench to indulge pity, but to administer justice ,
and while he was sorry for the offender, he would
never justify the offence.   " John," said he, " I am
surprised that you could for a moment forget that I
never accept any gift which causes the giver to break
a law.   On Sunday I teach you from the pulpit the
laws of God, whose minister I am.   At present I fill
the chair of the magistrate to enforce and execute the
laws of the land.   Between those and the others
there is more connexion than you are aware.   I thank
you, John, for your affection to me, and I admire your
gratitude ; but I must not allow either affection or
gratitude to be brought as a plea for a wrong action.
It is not your business nor mine, John, to settle
whether the game laws are good or bad.   Till they
are repealed we must obey them.   Many, I doubt
not, break these laws through ignorance, and many, I
am certain, who would not dare to steal a goose or a
turkey, make no scruple of knocking down a hare or
a partridge.   You will hereafter think yourself happy
that this your first attempt has proved unsuccessful,
as I trust you are too honest a fellow ever to intend
to turn poacher.   With poaching much moral evil is
connected ; a habit of nightly depredation ; a custom
of prowling in the dark for prey produces in time a
disrelish for honest labor.   He whose first offence was
committed without much thought or evil intention,
if he happens to succeed a few times in carrying off
his booty undiscovered, grows bolder and bolder ;
and when he fancies there is no shame attending it,
he very soon gets to persuade himself that there is
also no sin.   While some people pretend a scruple
about stealing a sheep, they partly live by plundering
  f warrens.   But remember that the warrener pays a

high rent, and that therefore his rabbits are as much his property as his sheep. Do not then deceive yourselves with these false distinctions. All property is sacred, and as the laws of the land are intended to fence in that property, he who brings up his children to break down any of these fences, brings them up to certain sin and ruin. He who begins with robbing orchards, rabbit-warrens, and fish-ponds, will probably end with horse-stealing or highway robbery. Poaching is a regular apprenticeship to bolder crimes. He whom I may commit as a boy to sit in the stocks for killing a partridge, may be likely to end at the gallows for killing a man.

"Observe, you who now hear me, the strictness and impartiality of justice. I know Giles to be a worthless fellow, yet it is my duty to take his information ; I know Jack Weston to be an honest youth, yet I must be obliged to make him pay the penalty. Giles is a bad man, but he can prove this fact ; Jack is a worthy lad, but he has committed this fault. I am sorry for you, Jack ; but do not let it grieve you that Giles has played worse tricks a hundred times, and yet got off, while you were detected in the very first offence, for that would be grieving because you are not as great a rogue as Giles. At this moment you think your good luck is very unequal ; but all this will one day turn out in your favor. Giles is not the more a favorite of Heaven because he has hitherto escaped Botany Bay or the hulks ; nor is it any mark of God's displeasure against you, John, that you were found out in your very first attempt."

Here the good justice left off speaking, and no one could contradict the truth of what he had said. Weston humbly submitted to his sentence, but he was very poor, and knew not where to raise the money to pay his fine. His character had always been so fair, that several farmers present, kindly agreed to advance a trifle each to prevent his being sent to prison, and he thankfully promised to work

out the debt. The justice himself, though he could
not soften the law, yet showed Weston so much
kindness that he was enabled before the year was out,
to get out of this difficulty. He began to think more
seriously than he had ever yet done, and grew to abhor
poaching, not merely from fear, but from principle.

We shall see whether poaching Giles always got
off so successfully. Worldly prosperity is no sure
sign of goodness. The " triumph of the wicked is
short."

History of Widow Brown's Apple-Tree.

As to Giles and his boys, old Widow Brown has
good reason to remember their dexterity. Poor
woman! she had a fine little bed of onions in her
neat and well-kept garden; she was very fond of her
onions, and many a rheumatism has she caught by
kneeling down to weed them in a damp day, notwithstanding the little flannel cloak and the bit of an old
mat which Madam Wilson gave her, because the old
woman would needs weed in wet weather. Her
onions she always carefully treasured up for her winter's store; for an onion makes a little broth very
relishing, and is indeed the only savory thing poor
people are used to get. She had also a small orchard,
containing about a dozen apple-trees, with which in
a good year she had been known to make a couple of
barrels of cider, which she sold to her landlord
toward paying her rent, besides having a little keg
which she was able to keep back for her own drinking. Well! would you believe it, Giles and his boys
marked both onions and apples for their own; indeed,
a man who stole so many rabbits from the warrener,
was likely enough to steal onions for sauce. One day
when the widow was abroad on a little business,
Giles and his boys made a clear riddance of the onion
bed; and when they had pulled up every single
onion, they then turned a couple of pigs into the
garden, who, allured by the smell, tore up the bed in

such a manner, that the widow, when she came home, had not the least doubt but the pigs had been the thieves. To confirm this opinion, they took care to leave the latch half open at one end of the garden, and to break down a slight fence at the other end.

I wonder how anybody can find in his heart not to pity and respect poor old widows. There is something so forlorn and helpless in their condition, that methinks it is a call on everybody, men, women, and children, to do them all the kind services that fall in their way. Surely their having no one to take their part, is an additional reason for kind-hearted people not to hurt and oppress them. But it was this very reason which led Giles to do this woman an injury. With what a touching simplicity is it recorded in scripture, of the youth whom our blessed Savior raised from the dead, that he was the only son of his mother, *and she a widow!*

It happened unluckily for poor Widow Brown that her cottage stood quite alone. On several mornings together, for roguery gets up much earlier than industry, Giles and his boys stole regularly into her orchard, followed by their jack-asses. She was so deaf that she could not hear the asses if they had brayed ever so loud, and to this Giles trusted; for he was very cautious in his rogueries, since he could not otherwise have contrived so long to keep out of prison: for though he was almost always suspected, he had seldom been taken up, and never convicted. The boys used to fill their bags, load their asses, and then march off; and if in their way to the town where the apples were to be sold, they chanced to pass by one of their neighbors who might be likely to suspect them, they then all at once began to scream out, "Buy my coal!—buy my sand!"

Besides the trees in her orchard, poor Widow Brown had in her small garden one apple-tree particularly fine; it was a red-streak, so tempting and so lovely, that Giles's family had watched it with longing eyes, till at last they resolved on a plan for carrying off all this fine fruit in their bags. But it was a nice point to manage. The tree stood directly under her chamber window, so that there was some danger that she might spy them at the work They therefore determined to wait till the next Sunday morning, when they knew she would not fail to be at church. Sunday came, and during service Giles attended. It was a lone house, as I said before, and the rest of the parish were safe at church. In a trice the tree was cleared, the bags were filled, the asses were whipped, the thieves were off, the coast was clear, and all was safe and quiet by the time the sermon was over.

Unluckily, however, it happened that this tree was so beautiful, and the fruit so fine, that the people, as they used to pass to and from the church, were very apt to stop and admire Widow Brown's red-streaks; and some of the farmers rather envied her that in that scarce season, when they hardly expected to make a pie out of a large orchard, she was likely to make a cask of cider from a single tree. I am afraid, indeed, if I must speak out, she herself rather set her heart too much upon this fruit, and had felt as much pride in her tree as gratitude to a good Providence for it; but this failing of hers was no excuse for Giles. The covetousness of this thief had for once got the better of his caution; the tree was too completely stripped, though the youngest boy Dick did beg hard that his father would leave the poor old woman enough for a few dumplings; and when Giles ordered Dick in his turn to shake the tree, the boy did it so gently that hardly any apples fell, for which he got a good stroke of the stick with which the old man was beating down the apples.

The neighbors on their return from church stopped as usual, but it was not, alas! to admire the apples, or apples there were none left, but to lament the robbery, and console the widow. Meantime the red-streaks were safely lodged in Giles's hovel, under a few bundles of new hay which he had contrived to pull from the farmer's mow the night before, for the use of his jack-asses. Such a stir, however, began to be made about the widow's apple-tree, that Giles, who knew how much his character had laid him open to suspicion, as soon as he saw the people safe in church again in the afternoon, ordered his boys to carry each a hatful of the apples, and thrust them in a little casement window which happened to be open in the house of Samuel Price, a very honest carpenter in that parish, who was at church with his whole family. Giles's plan, by this contrivance, was to lay the theft on Price's sons in case the thing should come to be further inquired into. Here Dick put in a word, and begged and prayed his father not to force them to carry the apples to Price's. But all that he got by his begging was such a knock as had nearly laid him on the earth. " What, you cowardly rascal," said Giles, " you will go and '*peach*, I suppose, and get your father sent to jail."

Poor Widow Brown, though her trouble had made her still weaker than she was, went to church again in the afternoon : indeed, she rightly thought that her being in trouble was a new reason why she ought to go. During the service she tried with all her might not to think of her red-streaks, and whenever they would come into her head, she took up her prayer-book directly, and so she forgot them a little ; and indeed, she found herself much easier when she came out of the church than when she went in, an effect so commonly produced by prayer, that methinks it is a pity people do not try it oftener. Now it happened oddly enough, that on that Sunday, of all the Sundays in the year, the widow should call in to rest a little at Samuel Price's, to tell over again the lamentable story of the apples, and to consult with him how the thief might be brought to justice. But O, reader!

guess if you can, for I am sure I can not tell you, what was her surprise, when, on going into Samuel Price's kitchen, she saw her own red-streaks lying on the window! The apples were of a sort too remarkable for color, shape, and size, to be mistaken. There was not such another tree in the parish. Widow Brown immediately screamed out, " Alas-a-day, as sure as can be, here are my red-streaks; I could swear to them in any court." Samuel Price, who believed his sons to be as honest as himself, was shocked and troubled at the sight. He knew he had no red-streaks of his own ; he knew there were no apples in the window when he went to church : he did verily believe these apples to be the widow's. But how they came there he could not possibly guess. He called for Tom, the only one of his sons who now lived at home. Tom was at the Sunday school, which he had never once missed since Mr. Wilson the minister had set up one in the parish. Was such a boy likely to do such a deed ?

A crowd was by this time got about Price's door, among which were Giles and his boys, who had already taken care to spread the news that Tom Price was the thief. Most people were unwilling to believe it. His character was very good, but appearances were strongly against him. Mr. Wilson, who had stayed to christen a child, now came in. He was much concerned that Tom Price, the best boy in his school, should stand accused of such a crime. He sent for the boy, examined, and cross-examined him. No marks of guilt appeared. But still though he pleaded *not guilty*, there lay the red-streaks in his father's window. All the idle fellows in the place, who were most likely to have committed such a theft themselves, were the very people who fell with vengeance on poor Tom. The wicked seldom give any quarter. " This is one of your sanctified ones!" cried they. " This was all the good that Sunday schools did! For their parts they never saw any good come by religion. Sunday was the only day for a little pastime, and if poor boys must be shut up with their godly books, when they ought to be out taking a little pleasure, it was no wonder they made themselves amends by such tricks." Another said he should like to see Parson Wilson's righteous one well whipped. A third hoped he would be clapped in the stocks for a young hypocrite as he was; while old Giles, who thought the only way to avoid suspicion was by being more violent than the rest, declared, that " he hoped the young dog would be transported for life."

Mr. Wilson was too wise and too just to proceed against Tom without full proof. He declared the crime was a heavy one, and he feared that heavy must be the punishment. Tom, who knew his own innocence, earnestly prayed to God that it might be made to appear as clear as the noonday; and very fervent were his secret devotions on that night.

Black Giles passed his night in a very different manner. He set off as soon as it was dark, with his sons and their jack-asses, laden with their stolen goods. As such a cry was raised about the apples, he did not think it safe to keep them longer at home, but resolved to go and sell them at the next town, borrowing without leave a lame colt out of the moor to assist in carrying off his booty.

Giles and his eldest sons had rare sport all the way in thinking, that while they were enjoying the profit of their plunder, Tom Price would be whipped round the market-place at least, if not sent beyond sea. But the younger boy Dick, who had naturally a tender heart, though hardened by his long familiarity with sin, could not help crying, when he thought that Tom Price might, perhaps, be transported for a crime which he himself had helped to commit. He had had no compunction about the robbery, for he had not been instructed in the great principles of truth and justice; nor would he therefore, perhaps, have had much remorse about accusing an innocent boy.

But though utterly devoid of principle, he had some remains of natural feeling and of gratitude. Tom Price had often given him a bit of his own bread and cheese; and once, when Dick was like to be drowned, Tom had jumped into the pond with his clothes on, and saved his life when he was just sinking; the remembrance of all this made his heart heavy. He said nothing; but as he trotted barefoot after the asses, he heard his father and brothers laugh at having outwitted the godly ones; and he grieved to think how poor Tom would suffer for his wickedness, yet fear kept him silent; they called him a sulky dog, and lashed the asses till they bled.

In the meantime Tom Price kept up his spirits as well as he could. He worked hard all day, and prayed heartily night and morning. "It is true," said he to himself, "I am not guilty of this sin; but let this accusation set me on examining myself, and truly repenting of all my other sins; for I find enough to repent of, though I thank God I did not steal the widow's apples."

At length Sunday came, and Tom went to school as usual. As soon as he walked in, there was a great deal of whispering and laughing among the worst of the boys; and he overheard them say, "Who would have thought it? This is master's favorite!—This is Parson Wilson's sober Tommy! We sha'n't have Tommy thrown in our teeth again if we go to get a bird's nest, or gather a few nuts on a Sunday." "Your demure ones are always hypocrites," says another. "The still sow suck all the milk," says a third.

Giles's family had always kept clear of the school. Dick, indeed, had sometimes wished to go; not that he had much sense of sin, or desire after goodness, but he thought if he could once read, he might rise in the world, and not be forced to drive asses all his life. Through this whole Saturday night he could not sleep. He longed to know what would be done

to Tom. He began to wish to go to school, but he
had not courage : sin is very cowardly. So on the
Sunday morning he went and sat himself down under
the church wall. Mr. Wilson passed by. It was
not his way to reject the most wicked, till he had
tried every means to bring them over ; and even then
he pitied and prayed for them. He had, indeed, long
left off talking to Giles's sons ; but seeing Dick sitting
by himself, he once more spoke to him, desired him to
leave off his vagabond life, and go with him into the
school. The boy hung down his head, but made no
answer. He did not, however, either rise up and run
away, or look sulky, as he used to do. The minister
desired him once more to go. "Sir," said the boy,
"I can't go ; I am so big I am ashamed."—"The
bigger you are the less time you have to lose."—
"But, sir, I can't read."—"Then it is high time you
should learn."—"I should be ashamed to begin to
learn my letters."—"The shame is not in beginning
to learn them, but in being contented never to know
them."—"But, sir, I am so ragged!"—"God looks
at the heart, and not at the coat."—"But, sir, I have
no shoes and stockings."—"So much the worse. I
remember who gave you both."—Here Dick colored.
"It is bad to want shoes and stockings ; but still, if you
can drive your asses a dozen miles without them, you
may certainly walk a hundred yards to school without
them."—"But, sir, the good boys will hate me, and
won't speak to me."—"Good boys hate nobody ; and
as to not speaking to you, to be sure they will not
keep your company while you go on in your present
evil courses ; but as soon as they see you wish to reform, they will help you, and pity you, and teach
you ; and so come along."—Here Mr. Wilson took
this dirty boy by the hand, and gently pulled him forward, kindly talking to him all the way in the most
condescending manner.

How the whole school stared to see Dick Giles
come in! No one, however dared to say what he

14

thought. The business went on, and Dick slunk into a corner, partly to hide his rags, and partly to hide his sin, for last Sunday's transaction sat heavy on his heart, not because he had stolen the apples, but because Tom Price had been accused. This, I say, made him slink behind. Poor boy! he little thought there was ONE saw him who sees all things, and from whose eye no hole nor corner can hide the sinner; "for he is about our bed, and about our path, and spieth out all our ways."

It was the custom in that school, and an excellent custom it is, for the master, who was a good and wise man, to mark down in his pocketbook all the events of the week, that he might turn them to some account in his Sunday evening instructions, such as any useful story in the newspaper, any account of boys being drowned as they were out in a pleasure-boat on Sundays, any sudden death in the parish, or any other remarkable visitation of Providence, insomuch, that many young people in the place, who did not belong to the school, and many parents also, used to drop in for an hour on a Sunday evening, when they were sure to hear something profitable. The minister greatly approved this practice, and often called in himself, which was a great support to the master, and encouragement to the people who attended.

The master had taken a deep concern in the story of Widow Brown's apple-tree. He could not believe Tom Price was guilty, nor dared he pronounce him innocent, but he resolved to turn the instructions of the present evening to this subject. He began thus: "My dear boys, however light some of you may make of robbing an orchard, yet I have often told you there is no such thing as a *little* sin, if it be wilful or habitual. I wish now to explain to you, also, that there is hardly such a thing as a *single* solitary sin. You know I teach you not merely to repeat the commandments as an exercise for your memory, but

as a rule for your conduct. If you were to come
here only to learn to read and spell on a Sunday, I
should think that was not employing God's day for
God's work, but I teach you to read that you may,
by this means, come so to understand the Bible and
the Catechism, as to make every text in the one, and
every question and answer in the other, to be so fixed
in your hearts that they may bring forth in you the
fruits of good living."

Master. How many commandments are there?

Boy. Ten.

Master. How many commandments did that boy
break who stole Widow Brown's apples?

Boy. Only one, master, the eighth.

Master. What is the eighth?

Boy. *Thou shalt not steal.*

Master. And you are very sure that this was the
only one he broke? Now suppose I could prove to
you that he probably broke not less than six out of
those ten commandments, which the great Lord of
heaven himself stooped down from his eternal glory
to deliver to men, would you not, then, think it a terrible thing to steal, whether apples or guineas?

Boy. Yes, master.

Master. I will put the case. Some wicked boy
has robbed Widow Brown's orchard. Here the eyes
of every one were turned on poor Tom Price, except
those of Dick Giles, who fixed his on the ground.
I accuse no one, continued the master, Tom Price is
a good boy, and was not missing at the time of the
robbery; these are two reasons why I presume that
he is innocent; but whoever it was, you allow that
by stealing these apples he broke the eighth commandment?

Boy. Yes, master.

Master. On what day were these apples stolen?

Boy. On Sunday.

Master. What is the fourth commandment?

Boy. Thou shalt keep holy the sabbath-day.

Master. Does that person keep holy the sabbath-day who loiters in an orchard on Sunday, when he should be at church, and steals apples when he ought to be saying his prayers?

Boy. No, master.

Master. What command does he break?

Boy. the fourth.

Master. Suppose this boy had parents who had sent him to church, and that he had disobeyed them by not going, would that be keeping the fifth commandment?

Boy. No, master, for the fifth commandment says, *Thou shalt honor thy father and thy mother.*

This was the only part of the case in which poor Dick Giles's heart did not smite him; he knew he had disobeyed no father—for his father, alas! was still wickeder than himself, and had brought him up to commit the sin. But what a wretched comfort was this! The master went on.

Master. Suppose this boy earnestly coveted this fruit, though it belonged to another person, would that be right?

Boy. No, master, for the tenth commandment says, *Thou shalt not covet.*

Master. Very well. Here are four of God's positive commands already broken. Now do you think thieves ever scruple to use wicked words?

Boy. I am afraid not, master.

Here Dick Giles was not so hardened but that he remembered how many curses had passed between him and his father while they were filling the bags, and he was afraid to look up. The master went on.

I will now go one step further. If the thief, to all his other sins, has added that of accusing the innocent to save himself, if he should break the ninth commandment, by *bearing false witness against a harmless neighbor,* then six commandments are broken for an *apple!* But if it be otherwise, if Tom Price should be found guilty, it is not his good character shall save him. I shall shed tears over him, but punish him I must, and that severely." "No, that you sha'n't," roared out Dick Giles, who sprung from his hiding-place, fell on his knees, and burst out a-crying; "Tom Price is as good a boy as ever lived; it was father and I who stole the apples!"

It would have done your heart good to have seen the joy of the master, the modest blushes of Tom Price, and the satisfaction of every honest boy in the school. All shook hands with Tom, and even Dick got some portion of pity. But while Mr. Wilson left the guilty boy to the management of the master, he thought it became him, as a minister and a magistrate, to go to the extent of the law in punishing the father. Early on the Monday morning he sent to apprehend Giles. In the meantime Mr. Wilson was sent for to a gardener's house two miles distant, to attend a man who was dying. This was a duty to which all others gave way in his mind. He set out directly, but what was his surprise, on his arrival, to see, on a little bed on the floor, poaching Giles lying in all the agonies of death! Jack Weston, the same poor young man against whom Giles had informed for killing a hare, was kneeling by him, offering him some broth, and talking to him in the kindest manner. Mr. Wilson begged to know the meaning of all this, and Jack Weston spoke as follows:—

"At four in the morning, as I was going out to mow, passing under the high wall of this garden, I heard a most dismal moaning. The nearer I came the more dismal it grew. At last, who should I see but poor Giles groaning, and struggling under a quantity of bricks and stones, but not able to stir. The day before he had marked a fine large net on this old wall, and resolved to steal it, for he thought it might do as well to catch partridges as to preserve cherries; so, sir, standing on the very top of this wall, and tugging with all his might to loosen the net from the hooks which fastened it, down came Giles, net, wall,

and all, for the wall was gone to decay. It was very
high, indeed, and poor Giles not only broke his thigh,
but has got a terrible blow on his head, and is bruised
all over like a mummy. On seeing me, sir, poor
Giles cried out, 'Oh, Jack! I did try to ruin thee by
lodging that information, and now thou wilt be revenged by letting me lie here and perish.' 'God forbid, Giles!' cried I; 'thou shalt see what sort of revenge a Christian takes.' So, sir, I sent off the gardener's boy to fetch a surgeon, while I scampered home
and brought on my back this bit of a hammock,
which is indeed my own bed, and put Giles upon it;
we then lifted him up, bed and all, as tenderly as if
he had been a gentleman, and brought him in here.
My wife has just brought him a drop of nice broth;
and now, sir, as I have done what I could for this
poor perishing body, it was I who took the liberty to
send to you to come to try to help his poor soul, for
the doctor says he can't live."

Mr. Wilson could not help saying to himself, "Such
an action as this is worth a whole volume of com-
ments on that precept of our blessed Master, *Love
your enemies ; do good to them that hate you.*" Giles's
dying groans confirmed the sad account Weston had
just given. The poor wretch could neither pray
himself nor attend to the minister. He could only
cry out, "Oh! sir, what will become of me? I don't
know how to repent. O my poor wicked children!
Sir, I have bred them all up in sin and ignorance.
Have mercy on them, sir; let me not meet them in
the place of torment to which I am going. Lord,
grant them that time for repentance which I have
thrown away!" He languished a few days, and died
in great misery—a fresh and sad instance that people
who abuse the grace of God, and resist his spirit,
find it difficult to repent.

Except the minister and Jack Weston, no one came
to see poor Giles, besides Tommy Price, who had
been so sadly wronged by him. Tom often brought

him his own rice-milk or apple-dumpling, and Giles,
ignorant and depraved as he was, often cried out,
that "he thought now there must be some truth in
religion, since it taught even a boy to *deny himself*,
and to *forgive an injury*. Mr. Wilson, the next Sunday, made a moving discourse on the danger of what
are called *petty offences*.

V. THE SERVANT MAN TURNED SOLDIER.

WILLIAM was a lively young servant, who lived in a *great but very irregular family.* His place was on the whole, agreeable to him, and suited to his gay thoughtless temper. He found a plentiful table and a good cellar. There was, indeed, a great deal of work to be done, though it was performed with much disorder and confusion. The family, in the main, were not unkind to him, though they often contradicted and crossed him, especially when things went ill with themselves. This William never much liked, for he was always fond of having his own way. There was a merry, or rather a noisy and riotous servant's hall; for disorder and quarrels are indeed the usual effects of plenty and unrestrained indulgence. The men were smart, but idle; the maids were showy but licentious, and all did pretty much as they liked for a time, but the time was commonly short. The wages were reckoned high, but they were seldom paid, and it was even said by sober people, that the family was insolvent, and never fulfilled any of their flattering engagements, or their most positive promises; but still, notwithstanding their real poverty, things went on with just the same thoughtlessness and splendor, and neither master nor servants looked beyond the jollity of the present hour.

In this unruly family there was little church-going, and still less praying at home. They pretended, indeed, in a general way, to believe in the Bible, but it was only an outward profession, few of them read it

at all, and even of those who did read it still fewer
were governed by it.   There was indeed a Bible lying
on the table in the great hall, which was kept for the
purpose of administering an oath, but was seldom
used on any other occasion, and some of the heads
of the family were of opinion that this was its only
real use, as it might serve to keep the lower parts of
it in order.

William, who was fond of novelty and pleasure,
was apt to be negligent of the duties of the house.
He used to stay out on his errands, and one of his
favorite amusements was going to the parade to see
the soldiers exercise.   He saw with envy how smartly
they were dressed, listened with rapture to the music,
and fancied that a soldier had nothing to do but to
walk to and fro in a certain regular order, to go
through a little easy exercise, in short, to live without
fighting, fatigue. or danger.

O, said he, whenever he was affronted at home,
what a fine thing it must be to be a soldier! to be so
well dressed, to have nothing to do but to move to
the pleasant sound of fife and drum, and to have so
many people come to look at one, and admire one.
O it must be a fine thing to be a soldier!

Yet when the vexation of the moment was over he
found so much ease and diversion in the great family,
it was so suited to his low taste and sensual appetites,
that he thought no more of the matter.   He forgot
the glories of a soldier, and eagerly returned to all
the mean gratifications of the kitchen.   His evil habits were but little attended to by those with whom he
lived; his faults, among which were lying and swearing, were not often corrected by the family, who had
little objection to those sins which only offended God
and did not much affect their own interest or property.
And except that William was obliged to work rather
more than he liked, he found little, while he was
young and healthy, that was very disagreeable in his
service.   So he went on, still thinking, however,

when things went a little cross, what a fine thing it was to be a soldier! At last one day as he was waiting at dinner, he had the misfortune to let fall a china dish, and broke it all to pieces. It was a curious dish, much valued by the family, as they pretended; this family were indeed apt to set a false fantastic value on things, and not to estimate them by their real worth. The heads of the family, who had generally been rather patient and good-humored with William, as I said before, for those vices, which though offensive to God did not touch their own pocket, now flew out into a violent passion with him, called him a thousand hard names, and even threatened to horsewhip him for his shameful negligence.

William in a great fright, for he was a sad coward at bottom, ran directly out of the house to avoid the threatened punishment; and happening just at that very time to pass by the parade where the soldiers chanced to be then exercising, his resolution was taken in a moment. He instantly determined to be no more a slave, as he called it; he would return no more to be subject to the humors of a tyrannical family; no, he was resolved to be free; or at least, if he must serve, he would serve no master but the king.

William, who had now and then happened to hear from the accidental talk of the soldiers that those who served the great family he had lived with, were slaves to their tyranny and vices, had also heard in the same casual manner, that the service of the king was *perfect freedom*. Now he had taken it into his head to hope that this might be a freedom to do evil, or at least to do nothing, so he thought it was the only place in the world to suit him.

A fine likely young man as William was, had no great difficulty to get enlisted. The few forms were soon settled, he received the bounty money as eagerly as it was offered, took the oaths of allegiance, was joined to the regiment and heartily welcomed by his new comrades. He was the happiest fellow alive. All was smooth and calm   The day happened to be very fine, and therefore William always reckoned upon a fine day. The scene was gay and lively, the music cheerful, he found the exercise very easy, and he thought there was little more expected from him.

He soon began to flourish away in his talk; and when he met with any one of his old fellow-servants, he fell a prating about marches and counter-marches, and blockades, and battles, and sieges, and blood, and death, and triumphs, and victories, all at random, for these were words and phrases he had picked up without at all understanding what he had said. He had no knowledge, and therefore he had no modesty; he had no experience and therefore he had no fears.

All seemed to go on swimmingly, for he had as yet no trial. He began to think with triumph what a mean life he had escaped from in the old quarrelsome family, and what a happy, honorable life he should have in the army. O there was no life like the life of a soldier!

In a short time, however, war broke out, his regiment was one of the first which was called out to actual and hard service. As William was the most raw of all the recruits he was the first to murmur at the difficulties and hardships, the cold and hunger, the fatigue and danger of being a soldier. O what watchings, and perils, and trials, and hardships, and difficulties, he now thought attended a military life! Surely, said he, I could never have suspected all this misery when I used to see the men on the parade in our town.

He now found, when it was too late, that all the field-days he used to attend, all the evolutions and exercises which he had observed the soldiers to go through in the calm times of peace and safety, were only meant to fit, train, and qualify them, for the actual service which they were now sent out to perform by the command of the king.

The truth is, William often complained when there was no real hardship to complain of; for the common troubles of life fell out pretty much alike to the great family which William had left, and to the soldiers in

the king's army. But the spirit of obedience, discipline, and self-denial of the latter, seemed hardships
to one of William's loose turn of mind. When he
began to murmur, some good old soldier clapped him
on the back, saying, "Cheer up, lad, it is a kingdom
you are to strive for; if we faint not, henceforth there
is laid up for us a great reward; we have the king's
word for it, man." William observed, that to those
who truly believed this, their labors were as nothing,
but he himself did not at the bottom believe it; and it
was observed, of all the soldiers who failed, the true
cause was that they did not really believe the king's
promise. He was surprised to see that those soldiers
who used to bluster and boast, and deride the assaults
of the enemy, now began to fall away; while such as
had faithfully obeyed the king's orders, and believed in
his word, were sustained in the hour of trial. Those
who had trusted in their own strength, all fainted on
the slightest attack; while those who had put on the
armor of the king's providing, the sword, and the shield,
and the helmet, and the breastplate, and whose feet
were shod according to order, now endured hardship as
good soldiers, and were enabled to fight the good fight.

An engagement was expected immediately. The
men were ordered to prepare for battle. While the
rest of the corps were so preparing, William's whole
thoughts were bent on contriving how he might de-
sert. But alas! he was watched on all sides, he
could not possibly devise any means to escape. The
danger increased every moment, the battle came on.
William, who had been so sure and confident before
he entered, flinched in the moment of trial, while his
more quiet and less boastful comrades prepared boldly
to do their duty. William looked about on all sides,
and saw that there was no eye upon him, for he did
not know that the king's eye was everywhere at once.
He at last thought he spied a chance of escaping, not
from the enemy, but from his own army. While he
was endeavoring to escape, a ball from the opposite
camp took off his leg. As he fell, the first word

which broke from him were, " While I was in my
duty I was preserved; in the very act of deserting I
am wounded." He lay expecting every moment to be
trampled to death; but as the confusion was a little
over, he was taken off the field by some of his own
party, laid in a place of safety, and left to himself
after his wound was dressed.

The skirmish, for it proved nothing more, was soon
over. The greater part of the regiment escaped in
safety. William in the meantime suffered cruelly
both in mind and body. To the pains of a wounded
soldier he added the disgrace of a coward, and the in-
famy of a deserter. " O," cried he, " why was I such
a fool as to leave the *great family* I lived in, where
there was meat and drink enough and to spare, only
on account of a little quarrel? I might have made up
that with them as we had done our former quarrels.
Why did I leave a life of ease and pleasure, where I
had only a little rub now and then, for a life of daily
discipline and constant danger? Why did I turn
soldier? O what a miserable animal is a soldier!"

As he was sitting in this weak and disabled condition, uttering the above complaints, he observed a
venerable old officer, with thin gray locks on his head,
and on his face deep wrinkles engraved by time, and
many an honest scar inflicted by war. William had
heard this old officer highly commended for his extraor-
dinary courage and conduct in battle, and in peace he
used to see him cool and collected, devoutly employed
in reading and praying in the interval of more active
duties. He could not help comparing this officer with
himself. " I," said he, " flinched and drew back,
and would even have deserted in the moment of peril,
and now in return, I have no consolation in the hour
of repose and safety. I would not fight then, I can
not pray now. O why would I ever think of being a
soldier?" He then began afresh to weep and lament,
and he groaned so loud that he drew the notice of the
officer, who came up to him, kindly sat down by him,

15

took him by the hand, and inquired with as much affection as if he had been his brother, what was the matter with him, and what particular distress, more than the common fortune of war it was which drew from him such bitter groans? " I know something of surgery," added he, " let me examine your wound, and assist you with such little comfort as I can."

William at once saw the difference between the soldiers in the king's army, and the people in the great family; the latter commonly withdrew their kindness in sickness and trouble, when most wanted, which was just the very time when the others came forward to assist. He told the officer his little history, the manner of his living in the great family the trifling cause of his quarrelling with it, the slight ground of his entering into the king's service. " Sir," said he, " I quarrelled with the family, and I thought I was at once fit for the army : I did not know the qualifications it required. I had not reckoned on discipline, and hardships, and self-denial. I liked well enough to sing a loyal song, or drink the king's health, but I find I do not relish working and fighting for him, though I rashly promised even to lay down my life for his service if called upon, when I took the bounty money and the oath of allegiance. In short, sir, I find that I long for the ease and the sloth, the merriment and the feasting of my old service ; I find I can not be a soldier, and, to speak truth, I was in the very act of deserting when I was stopped short by the cannon ball. So that I feel the guilt of desertion, and the misery of having lost my leg into the bargain."

The officer thus replied : " Your state is that of every worldly irreligious man. The great family you served is a just picture of the world. The wages the world promises to those who are willing to do its work are high, but the payment is attended with much disappointment; nay, the world, like your great family, is in itself insolvent, and in its very nature incapable of making good the promises, and of paying the high rewards which it holds out to tempt its credulous followers. The ungodly world, like your family, cares little for church, and still less for prayer; and considers the Bible rather as an instrument to make an oath binding, in order to keep the vulgar in obedience, than in containing in itself a perfect rule of faith and practice, and as a title deed to heaven. The generality of men love the world as you did your service, while it smiles upon them, and gives them easy work and plenty of meat and drink; but as soon as it begins to cross and contradict them, they get out of humor with it, just as you did with your service. They then think its drudgery hard, its rewards low. They find out that it is high in its expectations from them, and slack in its payments to them. And they begin to fancy, because they do not hear religious people murmur as they do, that there must be some happiness in religion. The world, which takes no account of their deeper sins, at length brings them into discredit for some act of imprudence, just as your family overlooked your lying and swearing, but threatened to drub you for breaking a china dish. Such is the judgment of the world! It particularly bears with those who only break the laws of God, but severely punishes the smallest negligence by which they themselves are injured. The world sooner pardons the breaking ten commandments of God, than even a china dish of its own.

"After some cross or opposition, worldly men, as I said before, begin to think how much content and cheerfulness they remember to have seen in religious people. They therefore fancy that religion must be an easy and delightful, as well as a good thing. They have heard that, *her ways are ways of pleasantness, and all her paths are peace;* and they persuade themselves that by this is meant worldly pleasantness and sensual peace. They resolve at length to try it, to turn their back upon the world, to engage in the service of God, and turn Christians, just as you resolved to leave your old service, to enter into the service of the king, and turn soldier. But as you quitted your place in a passion, so they leave the world in a huff. They do not count the cost. They do not calculate upon the darling sin, the habitual pleasures, the ease and vanities which they undertake by their new engagements to renounce, any more than you counted what indulgences you were going to give up when you quitted the luxuries and idleness of your place to enlist in the soldier's warfare. They have, as I said, seen Christians cheerful, and they mistook the ground of their cheerfulness; they fancied it arose, not because through grace they had conquered difficulties, but because they had no difficulties in their passage. They fancied that religion found the road smooth, whereas it only helps to bear with a rough road without complaint. They do not know that these Christians are of good cheer, not because the world is free from tribulation, but because Christ, their captain, has *overcome the world.* But the irreligious man, who has only seen the outside of a Christian in his worldly intercourse, knows little of his secret conflicts, his trials, his self-denials, his warfare with the world without, and with his own corrupt desires within.

"The irreligious man quarrels with the world on some such occasion as you did with your place. He now puts on the outward forms and ceremonies of religion, and assumes the badge of Christianity, just as you were struck with the show of a field day; just as you were pleased with the music and the marching, and put on the cockade and red coat. All seems smooth for a little while. He goes through the outward exercises of a Christian, a degree of credit attends his new profession, but he never suspects there is either difficulty or discipline attending it; he fancies religion is a thing for talking about, and not a thing of the heart and the life. He never suspects that all the psalm-singing he joins in, and the sermons he hears, and the other means he is using, are only as the exercises and the evolutions of the soldiers, to fit and prepare him for actual service; and that these means are no more religion itself, than the exercises and evolutions of your parade were real warfare.

"At length some trial arises; this nominal Christian is called to differ from the world in some great point; something happens which may strike at his comfort, his credit, or security. This cools his zeal for religion, just as the view of an engagement cooled your courage as a soldier. He finds he was only *angry* with the world, he was not *tired* of it. He was out of humor with the world, not because he had seen through its vanity and emptiness, but because the world was out of humor with him. He finds that it is an easy thing to be a fair-weather Christian, bold where there is nothing to be done, and confident where there is nothing to be feared. Difficulties unmask him to others; temptations unmask him to himself; he discovers, that though he is a high professor, he is no Christian; just as you found out that your red coat and your cockade, your shoulder-knot and your musket, did not prevent you from being a coward.

"Your misery in the military life, like that of the nominal Christian, arose from your love of ease, your cowardice, and your self-ignorance. You rushed into a new way of life, without trying after one qualification for it. A total change of heart and temper was necessary for your new calling. With new views and principles, the soldier's life would have been not only easy, but delightful to you. But while with a new profession you retained your old nature, it is no wonder if all discipline seemed intolerable to you.

"The true Christian, like the brave soldier, is supported under dangers by a strong faith that the fruits of that victory for which he fights will be safety and peace. But, alas! the pleasures of this world are present and visible; the rewards for which he strives are remote. He therefore fails, because nothing short of a lively faith can ever outweigh a strong present temptation, and lead a man to prefer the joys of conquest to the pleasures of indulgence."

VI. THE GENERAL JAIL DELIVERY.

THERE was in a certain country a great king, who was also a judge. He was very merciful, but he was also very just, for he used to say that justice was the foundation of all goodness, and that indiscriminate and misapplied mercy was, in fact, injustice. His subjects were apt enough, in a general way, to extol his merciful temper, and especially those subjects who were always committing crimes which made them particularly liable to be punished by his justice. This last quality they constantly kept out of sight, till they had cheated themselves into a notion that he was too good to punish at all.

Now it had happened a long time before, that this whole people had broken their allegiance, and had forfeited the king's favor, and had also fallen from a very prosperous state in which he had originally placed them, having one and all become bankrupts. But when they were over head and ears in debt, and had nothing to pay, the king's son most generously took the whole burden of their debts on himself, and, in short, it was proposed that all their affairs should be settled, and their very crimes forgiven, for they were criminals as well as debtors, provided only they would show themselves sincerely sorry for what they had done themselves, and be thankful for what had been done for them. A book was also given them, in which a true and faithful account of their own rebellion was written, and of the manner of obtaining the king's pardon, together with a variety of directions for their conduct in time to come, and in this book it was particularly mentioned, that after having lived a certain number of years in a remote part of the same king's country, yet still under his eye and jurisdiction, there should be a *grand assizes*, when every one was to be publicly tried for his past behavior; and after this trial was over, certain heavy punishments were to be inflicted on those who should have still persisted in their rebellion, and certain high premiums were to be bestowed as a gracious reward upon the penitent and obedient.

This king's court differed in some respect from our courts of justice, being a sort of court of appeal, to which questions were carried after they had been imperfectly decided in the common courts! And not merely outward sins, but sins of the heart also were brought to light and reserved for this great day. Among these were pride, and oppression, and envy, and malice, and revenge, and covetousness, and secret vanity of mind, and evil thoughts of all sorts, and all sinful wishes and desires. The *sins of the heart* were by far the most numerous sort of sins which were to come before this great tribunal, and these were to be judged by this great king in person, and by none but himself, because he alone possessed a certain power of getting at all secrets.

Now you may be ready to think, perhaps, that these people were worse off than any others, because they were to be examined so closely, and judged so strictly. Far from it; the king gave them a book of directions; and because they were naturally short-sighted he supplied them with a glass for reading it, and thus the most dim-sighted might see, if they did not willingly shut their eyes; but though the king *invited* them to open their eyes he did not *compel* them. Many remained stone blind all their lives with the book in their hand, because they would not use the glass, nor take the proper means for reading and understanding all that was written for them. The humble and sincere learned in time to see even that part of the book which was least plainly written, and it was observed that the ability to understand it depended more on the heart than the head; an evil disposition blinded the sight, while humility operated like an eye-salve.

Now it happened that those who had been so lucky as to escape the punishment of the lower courts, took it into their heads that they were all very good sort of people, and of course very safe from any danger at this *great assize.* This grand intended trial, indeed, had been talked of so much, and put off so long, for it had seemed long at least to these short-sighted people, that many persuaded themselves it would never take place at all; and far the greater part were living away, therefore, without ever thinking about it: they went on just as if nothing at all had been done for their benefit, and as if they had no king to please, no king's son to be thankful to, no book to guide themselves by, and as if the assizes were never to come about. But with this king *a thousand years were as a day, for he was not slack concerning his promises, as some men count slackness.* So, at length, the solemn period approached. The day came, and every man found that he was to be judged for himself; that all his secrets were brought out, and that there was now no escape, not even a short reprieve; and some of the worst of the criminals were got together, debating in an outer court of the grand hall; and there they passed their time, not in compunction and tears, not in comparing their lives with what was required in that book which had been given them, but they derived a fallacious hope by comparing themselves with such as had been more notorious offenders. One who had grown wealthy by rapine and oppression, but had contrived to keep within the letter of the law, insulted a poor fellow as a thief, because he had stollen a loaf of bread. "You are far wickeder than I was," said a citizen to his apprentice. "for you drank

and swore at the ale-house every Sunday night."
"Yes," said the poor fellow, "but it was your fault
that I did so, for you took no care of my soul, but
spent all your sabbaths in jaunting abroad or in rioting at home ; I might have learnt, but there was no
one to teach me; I might have followed a good example, but I saw only bad ones. I sinned against
less light than you did,"

I can not describe the awful pomp of the court, and
shall only notice a few who claimed a right to be
rewarded by the king, and even deceived themselves
so far as to think that his own book of laws would
be their justification. A thoughtless spendthrift ad-
vanced without any contrition, and said that he had
lived handsomely, and had hated the covetous, whom
God abhorreth ; that he trusted in that passage of
the book which said, that *covetousness was idolatry,*
and that he therefore hoped for a favorable sentence.
Now this man had left his wife and children in
want through his excessive prodigality. The judge
therefore immediately pointed to that place in the
book where it is written, *He that provideth not for
his household is worse than an infidel. He that liveth
in pleasure is dead while he liveth.* "Thou," said he,
"*in thy lifetime receivedst thy good things, and now
thou must be tormented.*" Then a miser, whom hunger and hoarding had worn to skin and bone, crept
forward, and praised the sentence passed on this extravagant youth, "and surely," said he, "since he is
condemned, I am a man that may make some plea to
favor. I have been so self-denying that I am certainly a saint; I have loved neither father nor mother,
nor wife nor children, to excess. In all this I have
obeyed the book of the law." Then the judge said,
"But where are thy works of mercy and thy labors
of love; see that family which perished in thy sight
last hard winter, while thy barns were overflowing ;
that poor family were my representatives; yet they
were hungry, and thou gavest them no meat. *Go to,*

*now, thou rich man, weep and howl for the miseries that
are come upon you."*

Then came up one with a most self-sufficient air.
He walked up boldly, having in one hand the plan of
an hospital which he had built, and in the other the
drawing of a statue, which was erecting for him in
the country that he had just left, and on his forehead
appeared, in gold letters, the list of all the public
charities to which he had subscribed. He seemed to
take great pleasure in the condemnation of the miser,
and said, "Lord, when saw I thee hungry and fed
thee not, or in prison and visited thee not? I have
visited the fatherless and widow in their affliction."
Here the judge cut him short, by saying, "True,
thou didst visit the fatherless, but didst thou fulfil
equally that other part of my command, 'to keep
thyself unspotted from the world.' Thou wast conformed to the world in many of its sinful customs ;
thou didst follow a multitude to do evil; thou didst
love the world and the things of the world ; and the
motive to all thy charities was not a regard to me but
to thy own credit with thy fellow-men. Thou hast
done everything for the sake of reputation, and now
thou art vainly trusting in thy deceitful works, instead
of putting all thy trust in my Son, who has offered
himself to be a surety for thee. Where has been
that humility and gratitude to him which was required
of thee. Thou wouldst be thine own surety; thou
hast trusted in thyself; thou hast made thy boast of
thine own goodness ; thou hast sought after and thou
hast enjoyed the praise of men, and verily I say unto
thee, 'thou hast had thy reward.'"

A poor diseased blind cripple, who came from the
very hospital which this great man had built, then fell
prostrate on his face, crying out, "Lord, be merciful
to me a sinner!" on which the judge, to the surprise
of all, said, "Well done, good and faithful servant."
The poor man replied, "Lord, I have done nothing."
"But thou hast 'suffered well,'" said the judge

'thou hast been an example of patience and meekness, and though thou hadst but few talents, yet thou hast well improved those few; thou hadst time; this thou didst spend in the humble duties of thy station, and also in earnest prayer; thou didst pray even for that proud founder of the hospital, who never prayed for himself; thou wast indeed blind and lame, but it is nowhere said, my son, give me thy feet, or thine eyes, but give me thy heart; and the few faculties I did grant thee were employed to my glory: with thine ears thou didst listen to my word, with thy tongue thou didst show forth my praise; 'enter thou into the joy of thy Lord.'"

There were several who came forward, and boasted of some single and particular virtue, in which they had been supposed to excel. One talked of his generosity, another of his courage, and a third of his fortitude; but it proved on a close examination, that some of those supposed virtues were merely the effect of a particular constitution of body; that others proceeded from a false motive, and that not a few of them were actual vices, since they were carried to excess; and under the pretence of fulfilling one duty, some other duty was lost sight of; in short, these partial virtues were none of them practised in obedience to the will of the king, but merely to please the person's own humor, or to gain praise, and they would not, therefore, stand this day's trial, for " he that had kept the whole law, and yet had wilfully and habitually offended in any one point, was declared guilty of breaking the whole."

At this moment a sort of thick scales fell from the eyes of the multitude. They could now no longer take comfort, as they had done for so many years, by measuring their neighbors' conduct against their own. Each at once saw himself in his true light, and found, alas! when it was too late, that he should have made the book which had been given him his rule of practice before, since it now proved to be the rule by which he was to be judged. Every one now thought himself even worse than his neighbor, because, while he only *saw* and *heard* of the guilt of others, he *felt* his own in all its aggravated horror.

To complete their confusion, they were compelled to acknowledge the justice of the judge who condemned them; and also to approve the favorable sentence by which thousands of other criminals had not only their lives saved, but were made happy and glorious beyond all imagination; not for any great merits which they had to produce, but in consequence of their sincere repentance, and their humble acceptance of the pardon offered to them by the king's son. One thing was remarkable, that while most of those who were condemned, never expected condemnation, but even claimed a reward for their supposed innocence or goodness, all who were really rewarded and forgiven were sensible that they owed their pardon to a mere act of grace, and they cried out with one voice " Not unto us, not unto us, but unto thy name be th praise!"

THE END.